DON SIMON

By

Simon Carroll

ISBN-13: 978-1543091113
ISBN-10: 1543091113

To the ladies and what might have been.
Anne Lawrence
Kate Lowney
Claudia Wyss.

CONTENTS

To the one and only Mr Geert Tromp,

wherever you are.

PROLOGUE

We have to start somewhere,

so here's where.

The temperature was 100 degrees Fahrenheit. I stank; my body was running with sweat, my armpits having turned into human fountains. The people there to meet me had insisted on a ban on sunglasses so the glare of the sun was blinding. I am pretty sure many of you at some point in your life have said to yourself, "What the hell am I doing here?" Well, I was standing under an old dilapidated airport hangar somewhere in South Africa at the laughingly titled Upington International airport. It may have been just about bearable if no one else was around as the sauna effect was helping me shed a few unwanted pounds.

Sadly, I was there to meet the soon to be ex-Nigerian Minister of Finance, who was accompanied by several large men with machine guns. Like workmen looking down a hole we were peering into several crates stuffed with one hundred dollar bills. In total there was close to $800 million. So whatever you were doing and wherever you were when you uttered, "Why me? Get me the hell out of here," it is fair to say in my humble opinion, my story may top yours.

The deal before last had supposed to have been the last. So why one more? Guess you get greedy or is it the danger, or the buzz? Who knows? Well, maybe my business partner does. However, that is not how things had started out. We had initially done what I had thought to be several legitimate deals when we first started doing business together. This was his way of seeing if he could trust me. Clearly this was the case as one day out of the blue a man I considered a friend told me not only was he was a criminal, he loved it.

Apparently his associates had given him the task of finding a man who could clean their money. Guess who fitted the bill?

It does not take Einstein to figure that out, does it? Without wishing to overload readers with questions, please just one more for now. What makes a reasonably good man decide to dip a toe into the world of crime? Easy. Loads and loads of money and get this, no risk.

So for those with style and good taste, stay tuned. The hare's running.

CHAPTER 1

The cost of crime

Thud, thud, thud. "Ah, call me big boy, Sally."

It is fair to say you cannot or should not ever get used to the man in the next room masturbating. Sadly, that is the reality of prison life, albeit an open prison, AKA a holiday camp to readers of the Daily Tory-graph. The one crumb of comfort that can be thrown to readers of a right-wing disposition is that none of their taxes are spent on soundproofing the paper-thin walls in the chalets – sorry, cells. The truth is they are actually rooms and there are no bars, and you have a key to your own door. Please do not tell anyone about this, it may get out, which is more or less what this tale is about. Smooth, huh!

So, where to begin if you want to start the story from the beginning? I am not sure where or when that is so try and stay with me. If you want to find out what happens at the end, go to the last five pages, duh, or if you want to go backwards and forwards and be thoroughly entertained, stay with us here.

The first question is, how did I end up in an open prison? I got caught. Ha bloody ha. By the way, you do not get to go straight there; first you have to suffer real prison. Bars, bullies, blaggers, braggers, and the threat of being buggered. You have to tough it out, trying your best to look hard until some well-meaning screw can get through the mountains of paperwork and categorise you. Yes, I did say well-meaning; some of the prison officers are okay.

For the uninitiated, prisoners are graded on how dangerous they are. Cat A is your resident psychopath. B is trickier to explain; the government define it as a person who does not need maximum security but for whom escape still needs to be very difficult. So it could be you, as everyone starts at B, which brings a whole new meaning to plan B.

Cat C cons are just losers – small-timers, habitual criminals nicking anything that is not nailed down. They never leave you alone inside, constantly asking to borrow things or asking for your uneaten apples. They call it grafting; most would call it scrounging, these saddos are beyond contempt. Blimey, could send this as 'written by Angry from Tunbridge Wells'.

Which brings us to category D and me. We are, of course, the crème de la crème of the criminal world. Wow, how clever are computers? Mine automatically put on those accent things on crème. See? It did it again. Huh, was crème just used to describe criminals? 'Bring back the Birch' (AoTW).

Anyway, where were we? Oh yes – Cat D. You see, the prison system has a system. It is the opposite of the academic one which is where the goal is A. The big D is the goal when you find yourself on the inside.

That means even a lip-wobbling, mouth-frothing convict can make it. Just say sorry a lot and go on a shitload of anger management courses. D also encompasses your gentleman thief, occasional celebrity, and of course not as clever as they think they are – white-collar criminals. The last on this list, would best describe myself.

All of the above does not explain what I was doing in prison but to wet your appetite for more so you read on. Back to prison very briefly. We will return later if you would like an appetiser. Some of the highlights are as follows:

A mad Irishman beating up another prisoner because he fed his duck.

The Easter church service when do-gooders had to sit with the lags. Talk about dropped jaws.

A female officer having sex with several inmates; she got caught with her trousers down.

There are also tales of fights, a failed hanging, sunbathing, dare I say a few laughs, and you have to hang around for the great milk debacle of HMP Forrest Bank.

Who am I? Letting the days go by.

So who is this superhero? In a previous life I was Simon, a mild-mannered banker. Minding my business, helping rich people stay that way with a bit of tax avoidance advice thrown in for good luck. As jobs go, fair to say there are much worse. So, guess we will finally get to the beginning. To reassure you, prison is not the end; it is close and in many ways serves as a warning, so hopefully things will become much clearer from here.

CHAPTER 2

I am a total banker

My day job was as a client investment manager in international wealth management. For those of you without money (most of you, sorry about that), banking is just another function on the hamster wheel of life. It is a slightly more pleasant experience for people with extra cash. They are called clients, for a start; they are showered with offers of ways to improve their wealth, given freebies such as access to holiday villas and wined and dined at cooperate functions. My job was to kiss these people's rear ends. If I do say myself, I did quite a reasonable job. Also one does accrue knowledge of the financial jungle. The downside is that most of your customers – sorry, clients – barely acknowledge your existence. Still, you get to play around with their cash and take the odd gamble. However, it does create the odd pang of jealousy. For example, one guy had an account with over half a million pounds in that he had forgotten all about. Half a million, for flip's sake.

It is hard not to wonder if someone does not

know that they have an account, would they really miss it? At the time while this did cross my mind, believe it or not it was simply not enough. Well, you try and run for the rest of your life on 500k. Do the math and get back to me. For those not punching buttons on a calculator, I am unable to name the bank I worked for. Could of course hint at it with some less than subtle clues like Black Horses or even less subtle clues such as the Queen's bank or the Bank of Jock-land. We could even rip off Geraint Anderson who used such names as Mighty Yank bank and Merde Bank in his book *City Boy*. It is actually not that important that you know the name of the bank. Also, though I may appear cocky at times during this tale it would be nice to put the past behind me, and last but not least, who needs a lawsuit?

Please do not go into panic mode if you do have a few quid; there are safeguards. If some frustrated member of staff gets dizzy looking at all the pound signs and triple digit numbers, the devil may tap them on the back, tempting them to dip their hand in the till. This can cause a blood-draining, vomit-inducing feeling of absolute disbelief when the client realises that their account is empty. There is an investigation from the banking equivalent of the Stasi. You are grilled, disembowelled, hung, drawn, and possibly quartered. When it becomes obvious to even the thickest of skulls that you would be a blinking idiot to steal your own dosh, the numbers return to the screen and your money is returned. For anyone who has been put through this tedious and gut-wrenching experience, you know better than most that it is not a quick process. Spoiler alert, none of my clients' cash was stolen. Feel it is important that you know this!

So, although banks are soulless institutions that a long time ago wished that they had not agreed to look after your money and have long ceased to care about the customer, it is still marginally safer to deposit your cash in them than put it under your mattress.

Feel we are losing our way here. Okay, focus. So, worked in a bank moving money around, advising clients and trying to keep my finger on the pulse. Before we continue with this, as it is necessary to the story, a quick ad for where we are off to. Dear reader, we will drive down the Pacific Highway, pop into Paris, hobnob in Holland, sunbathe in Spain and Singapore, dance in Dubai and much, much more.

As previously stated you have to wine and dine people quite a bit at big events, however, now and again you do bump into the odd interesting person.

It is said that you never know when you are going to meet someone who can undo your world. At the time it appears this is the one you have been waiting for. A chance to breathe, the promise of never-ending sun, fine food, five-star treatment, and freedom.

His name was/is Geert; other aliases include Stomp, Mr Tromp, Cruyff, Blondie, Erasmus, Frans, and a few more. If the names above are not clues in themselves he is Dutch, though does hold at least another five passports. However, feel confident that he is from the Netherlands as I have met his mother once or twice. He seemed to know so much about these things, so I guess we can call him a Charming Man.

Mr Tromp cannot fail to draw attention to himself; firstly, he is very tall and very blond, hence the nom de plume above. Secondly, he could be Rutger Hauer's stunt double. That name may mean something to fans of Blade Runner and The Hitcher. Think he did some gravelly voiceovers for Guinness in the 1990s as well. The actor, not Geert. Both cloggies, by the way. At this particular function he was also accompanied by an extremely striking African lady. Believe she was Nigerian, and as I negotiate myself around eggshells, I have to say this is not the normal plus one brought to these meet and greets.

After my sycophantic tour of the room massaging my clients' egos, our paths crossed. The usual pleasantries were exchanged and I asked him what he did, as you do. This is the best time, I think, to get the speech marks out. "As an Aquarius I carry the water from one person to the next." Breathe for effect, drink a little tonic water. "There are some people, my new friend, who live in a dream world, and there are some who face reality, and then there is me who can turn one into the other." Enigmatic to say the least, though as they were not nailed down, sure those words may have been nicked from someone or other.

Before we move on, what do we think about starting the book with these quotes? Answers on a postcard please. Scratch that and delete if you want.

To paraphrase, my new friend was very amiable and I was also impressed that he had no desire to quaff as much free champagne as possible, like most in the room. Mr B. just gently nursed his tonic water while we talked. After exchanging business cards we agreed to meet again. His parting words were insisting that we could do business together, and also one final titbit of wisdom telling me opportunities do not just happen, you create them. One last quote from our new friend. "If you are not willing to risk the unusual then you have to settle for the ordinary."

Now, Mr or Ms Reader, you might wonder why it was not possible to see through these words. All that can be added is that with any success one has had, listen respectfully to the very best advice and then go away and do the exact opposite. So please do not take this the wrong way, but bollocks to the lot of you. It seemed a good idea at the time. Remember, Fortune favours the audacious. Now I know you know that is from the Dutch writer Erasmus; if you don't it is okay, however, you should read more!

So, where were we? Oh yes, me and the dodgy, devious Dutch man. After our first chat we met up a few times to discuss doing business (fictional on his side). It was pleasant to have someone who seemed interested in my work. None of my friends or family were, not even my wife. By the way, I was married at the time. As you read on it will become obvious that even the most loving of ladies would cut the cord. Still, she was and is okay.

As we have done the whole procrastination quote, it is fair to say that I may digress from time to time. What more can I say? All apologies.

Back to the meetings. For those who have to attend them, you know the scene; very humdrum, boredom, boredom, boredom, b'dum, b'dum. Big However. Mr T. was no fool. Whenever we met, it was never in anything as mundane as an office. First we would dine out, normally a routine because all the effort listening to clients resulted in loss of your appetite. Geert though, seemed to not only know the best places to go but the chefs as well. As he told me, when you get to know the chef you will start to enjoy dining out more. Our roles were reversed, with me doing the talking. After about a few meals we did what appeared to be a genuine deal. It was a simple transfer of funds from a Dutch company to an English subsidiary. All seemed above board and nice and legal. For some reason he was impressed with my part and the ease at which the transaction was accomplished. I also convinced the powers that be to waive the commission fee by telling them more lucrative deals lay further down the pipeline. The grasping greedy idiots licked their lips in anticipation and shook my hand warmly, there may also have been a pat on the back and a, "Go and get him."

As a thank you, our friendly Dutch man laid on an all-expenses paid trip to Paris for me and the missus. See, we do pop into Paris.

CHAPTER 3

So it begins

If you have never been to Paris before, you must. Sod ISIS, it is marvellous. There is an overwhelming air of good living and passionate individualism which you soak in just by sitting quietly over a fine glass of wine in a bistro. Mrs C. loved it too (AKA my wife). She is an art graduate and sees herself as a culture vulture. She started our trip quoting to me that one cannot escape the past in Paris. It intermingles so intangibly with the present that is never a burden. Oh, you have to love her. We dined at Maxim's, danced in the White Room, smiled at Mona and finally rested our heads on the plump pillows of the Ritz. Très magnifique. It is fair to say that even the most humble of humans feels like they dwell in paradise when in Paris. While sipping divine coffee (so smooth) waiting for my good lady to finish packing, I bumped into Blondie. Have to use all the aliases; he would be extremely disappointed otherwise. Believe it or not, at the time this did not raise any alarm bells.

Anyway, after exchanging pleasantries and

ordering another coffee – trust me, one is not enough – Blondie asked if I needed to get the okay to do another transfer. "Why would I?" was my reply. Gut!

After refusing breakfast and coming out with some crap about starving being considered art in Paris, we shook on the deal, he insisted that that commission was taken, and off he went.

Just a quick heads-up – did not think that line so bad at the time, in fact could not suppress a smile if the truth be told.

Back in the UK though, the transfer went through; the amount was quite a bit more than agreed. This, it appears, was just a sizing-up exercise of yours truly. A test of honesty, if that is not an oxymoron.

Need another breather? Can offer you a 20/20 cricket update. No? Okay. Hopefully any editor worth their salt will take these things out, unless we are doing a James Joyce here and changing the very theme of the narrative. Let us move on.

After discussing the amount with my client (AKA you-know-who) everything was hunky dory. The bank made a sizable commission and my back was raw from all the slapping. It appears that when it comes to making a quick quid the devil has taken a leave of absence from the detail as far as the higher-ups are concerned. The company had a new account and had already made two biggish deals and far from being idle, they wanted more, more, more.

Several deals and social events followed, much to the company's delight. So much so that they told me, "Bring out the big guns, give this guy everything we have." So what do they come up with? Football.

Bloody hell, how original. The bank had access to several executive boxes at Premier League clubs around the country, with plenty of prawn sandwiches prepared for the new upmarket fan (thanks to Roy Keane). Having been told to pick the most glamorous fixture, I contacted Geert. Guess what? He was made up about this.

Who knew? My employees had got something right. After getting over that shock we met at an Arsenal v Chelsea game. Some of players involved had been seen in the orange shirt of the Netherlands so it was a no-brainer. The game itself has long ago disappeared from my memory. Read *Fever Pitch* or ask Nick Hornby if you want to know the result, scorers, and attendance. The main purpose was another dalliance with my new best friend. Once again, he was charm personified and despite the absence of alcohol at his request, we had quite a few laughs. The lack of booze was not a problem on my side either, as according to the much-maligned lads' mag *Loaded*, it makes you sloppy. I read this in their 'How to be a Geezer' guide and tend to agree with them.

Several topics other than work were discussed and it is fair to say that a good time was had by all. In fact I am surprised the executive box was not on fire as we were getting on so well. To be honest – ha, that word again – it was a surprise to discover that GT liked football so much. Apparently he had played professionally in the Dutch Second Division and one season at Watford. Now even the most naive person might have struggled with the validity of his statement. My problem was, a fair few years of listening to clients drone on about their success had dampened my inquisitive side. The main thing is, why would you lie about playing for Watford? Sorry Elton, no need to go breaking your heart on this fact. Besides, this came from the mouth of a man who had been dipped in and marinated in self-confidence from an early age. So why lie about a minor achievement at most, just to impress someone? Google the Watford squads of the 1980s and look for Geert Tromp if you think it will make you feel better. The name may or may not appear, who knows? Personally, I never want to find out one way or another.

After the game, as the night was relatively young in a yummy mummy type way, we went on to a casino. The cash was flashed, both of us wishing to outdo each other in a friendly way. There may have been no champagne but the banter was in full flow. The bets got bigger and greater risks were taken. However, though, like a fat kid in a takeaway the chips kept coming our way. If a white flag was available it would have been hoisted above the building. The house did not just lose, if it were a fight the referee would have stopped it.

Once in the night air as we walked along the road with an independent air, you could almost hear the girls declare they must be millionaires, as they have just broke the bank at Mint Casino (note for tourists – the casino is in South Kensington). As a result of this triumph against the odds our friendship was well and truly cemented. Normally in a client relationship there is a field full of bullshit, however, my talent was somehow ensuring my group of clients stayed loyal. It also seemed they liked being in the same room as me. My latest fling, though, while not that terrible modern phrase, a 'Bromance', was different.

Just like the tonic water he drank, Erasmus was a great mixer and easy to take. Above all, our meeting business, or socials, were fun. Before we both went our separate ways another deal was proposed with the even better news that the meeting to dot the I's and cross the T's would be held in Old Amsterdam. It was also stressed that only if this was convenient. Who was I to disagree?

CHAPTER 4

An offer hard to refuse

My brother had lived in Amsterdam and whenever I had visited the city it had felt vibrant and alive. Now, to some visitors Amsterdam is just a city of sin. However, in my opinion the place is all about freedom and choice. So I guess you have the freedom to sin or at least can choose which inner voice you listen to, good or bad. In my book it was all good, so, ticket please.

Before we pack our bags, endure endless queues at the airport, then finally fasten our seatbelt, a client tale. Jean Pierre, a French client of mine (really), told me that his company allowed them to claim expenses for female escorts and even turned a blind eye to a visit to the massage parlour. He even offered me this particular hands-on experience at our last get-together. Now it is a little too early to say if this is a good book or not, but if I may I would like to get into yours. These type of goings on do not really do it for me. Believe it or not, my wife was the only one for me. So, while you can snigger about a trip to the

Dam, no one had to get their hands dirty. So, hope I am on the credit side of the ledger.

So now we are off to Amsterdam. A quick heads-up, if you ever choose or can afford to fly business class do not bother for flights less than three hours. Still, it does mean that you get off the plane first and breeze past customs. Having arrived early I spent the morning just people watching, something that never seems to lose its appeal, especially in foreign climes. There is also a pleasant feeling of anonymity when you are in another country. Time, though, like the proverb says does not wait for any man, so I had to run to meet our Cruyff-loving Dutch man. Like his idol, he had always stressed the importance of perfect timing.

Breezing into the café where we had arranged to meet, he plonked a large brown (it is the rule) paper bag in front of me, saying, "Simon, today is the perfect day to start living your dreams. You can fake your way to the table but you have to learn to eat and you have."

He then informed me that crime was his true love and his real business. It appears he was looking for special kind of business partner. What was a man to do? What indeed?

You may have your own opinion on crime, so let us start there. Is all crime wrong? If that is the case then no more breaking the speed limit, parking where you like and buying dodgy cigs down the pub. Also, consider this. Is stealing to eat criminal? Plus, I am not stealing to be rich, just cleaning. Too simplistic? Maybe so. The truth is I do not know. Like most people, hopefully, do have a sense of what is right and wrong, I still have to say in many ways, I could have said no to the offer. Feel like this is a cry for redemption, not sure. It did not seem so wrong then!

Anyway, Geert told me today he was Frans, another hero of his it seems. Some Dutch-Flemish painter or other. Today he was going to paint me a picture of being rich and the freedom it will bring, however, it was going to be an endeavour only for the strong hearted.

At this point I tried my best to show no emotion and decided just to listen. Quite easy to do when you are English. He explained that his associates needed help with moving their cash around. They needed to launder money; I feel an explanation coming up. This is when criminals disguise the original ownership and control of the proceeds of criminal conduct by making such proceeds appear to have derived from a legitimate source. Basically, making illegally gained proceeds (i.e. 'dirty money') appear legal (i.e. 'clean'). Apparently and unbelievably they had used couriers to move cash around the world. They had given various friends and acquaintances bags of cash to move from one country to another. Wow, as you can imagine this had become the home of Mr and Mrs Cock-Up. Strange then, that a bag of cash was not sat in front of me. Leaving that aside for now, the deal was if I was able to clean the cash legally and more successfully than the previous cack-handed efforts my end was 15% of every deal done. Just to whet your appetite, the first deal was one million US dollars so that is 150k to start – please think about that for a sec!

I broke my silence to ask as delicately as possible what sort of crime Mr Blondie loved.

He flashed a smile and asked if I trusted him. A

strange question in the current circumstances, but still, go on. For starters, did you know I was a smart guy? It is true, ask Frans if you do not believe me. Anyway, it appears the group faked a few insurance claims and had taken out loans with some finance companies they had no intention of repaying. Amazingly they had also received money for some government contracts that they had manged to somehow win for which they were being paid way over the odds for. There was some low-level bribery but nothing for me to worry about. Nor should I be concerned about any of the above. Get this, my name would never be used or known by anyone. Not only am I smart, I am also a good guy. "Simon, just help us once, see how it goes and then take one deal at a time. NO RISK!"

Pause for thought, all of you, please. There is also 50,000 dollars in a bag in front of me. The first 5%. Nice. Throw in a nice ambiance, good coffee, and an Enigmatic Dutch Man, it was very hard to resist. Before you rush to judge, think! No more setting alarm clocks or God forbid thinking about work. Oh yes, work, how much do you get a year then, eh? Come on. Well $150,000 is three years' salary for most people. Put that in your pipe and smoke it.

Though money is neither my god nor my devil it appears greed is a bottomless pit that I was about to fall into. There is a very fine line between wanting freedom and money and being greedy for it. Still, 150k! So, thinking more about the money than listening, it was only when I heard Geert say, "Can you help us or not? We need you. Plus, think of all the easy money," that my senses returned. It seems he saw me as a cool, calm guy who he wanted to keep a cool head, maintain a low profile, never taking the lead but still able to help do something big. So, never wanting to disappoint, I said yes. How could one refuse?

The next question was very fast. He asked how the money would be cleaned. Hmm, this was an easy one. Much more so than the first. There will be a crisis of conscience in the hotel later so please give me a break for now. Deals with God, plans to help the poor, homeless, etc...

CHAPTER 5

A sleepless night for me

Time to blind Blondie with science first. Act now, repent and think later.

I explained that this could be set up in three steps: placement, layering, and integration. First, the illegitimate funds are furtively introduced into the legitimate financial system. Then, the money is moved around to create confusion, sometimes by wiring or transferring through numerous accounts. Finally, it is integrated into the financial system through additional transactions until the 'dirty money' appears 'clean'. A piece of cake arrived at the table, it seemed apt. Our Dutch man was impressed, saying while he may be Frans Hals, I could be Rembrandt. This is not an attempt to appear highbrow. Geert, Stomp, Mr Tromp, Cruyff, Blondie, Erasmus, and Frans does dole these things out. They are on tap and maybe in quoting others, we cite ourselves. For art fans, if you see a Frans Hals painting it can encourage you to start painting. On viewing Rembrandt's work you would just give up.

Have to big myself up from time to time. The money in the bag was my mine, the million in cash was theirs for me to clean. So quid pro quo except it was in dollars. For those with any knowledge of banking, I do not need to tell you that you cannot just pop down to the High Street bank, and pop a million in. So, first things first, I would need to be in town for a while.

Funny when you see all of this you have to say, "What the hell!"

Speaking of hell, before we go there mentally, some quotes. Further instructions will follow.

Fools rush in where angels fear to tread.

Greed is more gullible than innocence.

The opposite of bravery is not cowardice, it is conformity.

Man is free at the moment he wishes to be.

Stupidity combined with arrogance and a huge ego will get you a long way.

There is no sin except stupidity.

Just one more. There are far better things ahead than I leave behind.

So please, pick one then decide how you feel about the tale so far. You can change your mind later if you like – no pressure.

Back to the problem in hand. The office expected me back that day, as did my good lady. Shit. What to do, what to do? Any advice? Thought not. Okay, so stay one night, make some plans then come back next week. By the way, I was still with Blondie at this point, hoped my anguish was not apparent. Nah, cool as. Told him I had to get back to the UK but would be back the following Monday to start the process. So now we are partners in crime. Time to turn the wheel of illusion. Mr T. was beside himself with joy; he told me in terms of our new partnership that we would commute across the world, living the dream. Okay, see you Monday then – same place, same time. I will be the man with the plan. Believe the phrase we are looking for is that he left grinning like a Cheshire Cat. So just me, a cake, a coffee, and 50k; had worse days.

Where to start? Easy part first. Called the office and fed them a line about a minor hiccup.

Do you think they minded? Not a bit. They were expecting £25,000 commission so they could wait for it, and me. Told them I would be in by lunch the following day. Great. See? Easy.

Next, the missus. A little trickier; after all, I'm in Amsterdam. The one thing in my favour is that she loved and trusted me. My, this is hard. My stomach is twisted with the guilt of what an arse I was. As the mop tops sang, better not to care too much for money, as money can't buy you love. Deep breath. She loves you and you her. So I dialled the number, surprised but pleased when she answered after just two rings. See? She does love me. Plus, I did not want to wait to speak to her. She asked me if everything was okay. Ah, that female ability to sense when all is not well. Explained everything was fine except I have to stay in this hell hole until the morning. Nobody is buying that, are they? I did phrase it in a nonchalant, joking way so we both laughed about this.

She asked if it was boring business. What a girl. "What else?" was my less inspired reply. She told me window shopping only – ah, of course – then dragged out my favourite line for her. I informed her that I would be too busy counting my blessings to do anything else. Always a winner and once again it did the trick, so we ended on a happy note. What more could you want from a phone call?

Two minor calls to change my flight and book a hotel then the rest of the day lay ahead in which to think. Fancy a 'for and against' list? Well, here is mine.

For – just the one, easy money.

Against – lies, jeopardy, crime, danger, the risk, and so on.

Still, the money. The rest of the day was taken up by this list with 'for' still ahead even though the 'against' list grew and grew. Easy money, easy money, and guess what, easy money. Oh dear, hard to get past that.

Completely forgot to soak in the sights and sounds of Amsterdam, I just wandered around oblivious to everything. Finally, at around 10pm I checked into my hotel. A sleepless night lay ahead so I quickly sent a text wishing my wife sweet dreams. Was tempted to call, as I really wanted to tell her that I was thinking about her and that she was a such a star. However, I feared my voice may give the game away, so settled for cyberspace. Within seconds my phone flashed with a kiss symbol, a small comfort before the battle of my conscience. The 'for and against' list had been less than useless, so I thought about what the outcomes could be. Sadly, like William Blake, all that seemed to lie ahead was the road of excess leading to the palace of wisdom...You never know what is enough until you know what is more than enough.

Bloody hell, looks like I was in. Just for the record I was less than halfway along life's path so had the overwhelming desire to make the rest of the journey easy. After all, life is hard as it kills everybody in the end. Asked God, he was not in so it must be okay. Before turning into Easy Street first I have to tidy up 1.1 million in cash – easier said than done, despite my earlier protestations.

The biggest problem is that criminals love cold hard cash. They love the feel, the bundles, flashing it, and best of all throwing it around. Sadly, banks hate it and more importantly the police, customs, and governments are deeply suspicious of large amounts of it. So unless you fancy an anal search and hours and hours of questioning it is best to transfer money electronically. My mantra was that the fastest and easiest way to accomplish any task is to do it with minimum breaks and pauses. The use of offshore accounts is the best way to keep money hidden from the eyes of tax authorities, regulators, and nosy parkers. You can also use banks, law firms, trusts, and offshore shell companies to hide assets. The best part about this is you can take advantage of local banking and corporate laws to help hide the true identity of the owner of the money or other assets in the accounts. All of this makes it harder for authorities to link the money to the individual. See, give a hard job to a lazy man and he is sure to find an easy way of doing it.

The morning arrived. It seemed strange, almost out of place, though did remind me of the dreams I had been chasing, so I think it will be possible to make this pay. These days, you can take care of all of this and use outward deception to get away. After all, it is a modern age. So please stay for these days (thanks to the late great Ian Curtis, though did paraphrase a little). Okay then, I can do all the IT stuff in the UK, still just the teeny tiny problem of depositing a huge sum of money. Think. Who do we do business with in Holland?

Wait a minute. Scroll up. Shell companies. Ha! What about Royal Dutch Shell? Perfect. Petrol stations, cash, plus it is my fucking account, je suis un genie. The rest should have been history – just the one job, remember. If only.

Hello Simon, How are you doing? How are you feeling? Where are you staying? Hope you are okay, as you are aware I do really love you. Love Anne.

As mentioned before, you may now change your opinion at any given time. Oh, just takes me back to when my wife (just girlfriend at that point) and I were in our first place, young and dating. Many a night spent listening to Mazzy Star sitting in our room with the lights out under the blue glow of a beer light we picked up at a garage sale. Wow, sad how time has gone by so fast! It could be like those carefree days again. Concentrate. Think about the potential house on the beach, easy living, good wine, fine food, long walks, no pressure and freedom. Breezy but warm nights, the sky is royal blue and I can see all the stars as I lay on a quilt in the lush sand holding Anne's hand. Everything is calm and I am okay. The answer, it appears, is written. Man risks all for money. Oh well, here goes.

CHAPTER 6

Don't stop me now

Back in the UK. Though no one was the wiser to any change in my behaviour, one thing was troubling me. By going down the path I had chosen it would mean losing a customer. This would lead to a lot of awkward questions that I would not really be able to answer. Bugger.

After all, this was supposed to be my legitimate job, keeping clients and making money for the bank. In order to complete the dodgy deal it was extremely important that I had access to the bank's contacts and computers, so what to do? What to do? Maybe, maybe could do another deal with GT and with a little creative accountancy could move 25k from my cut into the bank's coffers and fake the deal, maybe even another. That that would solve the brown bag problem. After all, it was currently just sitting in a locker at Amsterdam railway station.

I would still be up by a $100,000 plus my share of the bank's commission, and still in grace and favour with all and sundry. Almost too good to be true. Already this may seem complicated to the outside observer, as well as bloody ridiculous. Well, when you get served the dream you have to expect the plate to be dammed hot.

Better plough on then. As previously mentioned, easy peasy lemon squeezey to do all the IT stuff, plus I had contacts with Shell and a colleague mentioned that we had just bought a currency firm, guess where? No, this cannot be true. Oh yes, the Netherlands. Who is helping me here? Better not to enquire further. Best of all they have a huge cash transfer system at Schiphol Airport where all the currency deals cash-wise go through. Hard as this is to believe, it is true as the Y at the end of the day. Touched by the hand of God on a sunny day. You really could not make this stuff up. Best of all, I would only have to be in Dutch land one or two days to oversee this. The Dutch did all the heavy lifting so to speak. Cash deposited, computers booted, and the wheels began to turn. Even had time for a dinner with an ecstatic Blondie and two divine companies, think one was for me (Blondie is my favourite name of his, though Geert has a certain style), however, he was not over concerned, when his generous offer of dessert was declined (please give me this).

I had agreed another deal – two million this time – blinded by the sun. Not only was he excited about the smooth money transfers, he had a two for one deal in more ways than one. Alea iact est. An irrevocable decision has been made. The die was cast and the damage was done. All you can do now is let it roll, you gotta roll, roll, roll all night long. For as Mr

Morrison says, "the future is uncertain and the end is always near."

You think this would be our happy ending. Think again. Despite myself I am extremely competent at what I do and first you may think two deals will be all. Sadly, like devious supermarkets' misleading multibuy deals, you know that the two for one, or BOGOF if you prefer, is nonsense.

Some final banking details for you. I had set up a shell company, which lacked any real operations and existed mainly on paper. It was not necessary jurisdiction-wise to identify an owner. The company had no person linked to it, which allowed me to control the account indirectly, through the company, and makes it harder for authorities to link the money to man or beast. This is astonishingly not illegal and unsurprisingly facilitates money laundering and helps conceal corruption and other such shenanigans.

It is also useful to brush up on your geography skills as you can take your pick from a whole heap of countries, such as Panama, the Cayman Islands, and Bermuda. There also are havens like the Isle of Man off Britain, Singapore, Macau off China, and the Cook Islands in the South Pacific. Some European countries like Switzerland and Luxembourg and principalities like Lichtenstein and Monaco also have banking laws which are designed to vigorously protect account owners' identities. The Caymans, for example, "has a well-deserved reputation for being a money-laundering and tax-evasion haven." The country's banking laws made it more difficult for law enforcement to investigate and prosecute cases of criminal activity. The anonymity afforded by shell companies and offshore accounts allowed me and other international criminals to hide and move money. Guess I have to group myself in with criminals now. These companies and accounts are an ideal vehicle for companies and – gulp – me again, who want to keep transactions secret to escape from all law enforcement agencies. Next time the financial news is on you are welcome to any of the above information. Change your name to J.P. Morgan, reel out some of this bumph as it may dazzle your partner, get you a promotion, stick it to a yuppie at a dinner party or hopefully get you some sexual action. Please do not hold your breath though. Still, may help you sleep.

Wake up! It is nearly time to change our name to Thomas Cook. So dig out your passport, get your vaccinations up to date, we will be off soon.

Meanwhile Geert, Stomp, Mr Tromp, Cruyff, Blondie, Erasmus, Frans, and the rest of the band were like men who had fallen into a barrel of breasts. He called his associates the G-men. During another memorable night at our favourite casino I did inform him that this term was used by special agents of the United States government, specifically the Federal Bureau of Investigations.

"Who?"

"That's the FBI, you daft Dutchman."

Believe he laughed like a drain. Oh, what joy. Oh, what fun. Guess we were about to have our season in the sun.

We had really bonded over the first deal and as much as I may dislike myself now, it was a thrill and somehow outwitting work and the authorities, to use a Manchester expression, had left me and Geert buzzing. So, agreeing to a second and in reality more, was a no-brainer. Since the first mad cash dash round the Dam, things had clicked and the transfers were working like clockwork. That was not only ironic but handy as the first point of call for most of the funds and our first trip together, was Switzerland. Orson Wells may feel the Swiss may have only contributed the cuckoo clock to the world, however, my associates and myself would strongly disagree. For a start there is an unlimited amount of numbered accounts, a one thousand franc note (£700), very handy for cash-loving crims, no curiosity and secrecy. Throw in clean air, great scenery, and numerous classy gifts to take home to the wife. People who deal in money see it as a small paradise in the middle of Europe. Mind you, in fairness to Mr Wells this is based on safety, cleanliness, political and economic stability. Not quite Ibiza but I liked it a great deal.

In regard to Zurich, I very much appreciated the cultural and gastronomic diversity of the city – and the many opportunities for enjoyment, recreation, and relaxation for all the senses. Picture if you will, a chocolate-box view of the city. The clear, glistening water of Lake Zurich with a magnificent view of the snow-capped mountains of the Alps in the distance. The place is pure class. We were there to access some of the clean cash, make sure there was no trail and then splash a bit of it about.

We arrived on a Thursday and our luxury-loving Dutchman had booked us into the Baur au Lac of FIFA fame – pure, pure opulence. Have I told you what great company GT is? Sure I did. Well, it does not hurt to repeat it. He really is great fun to be around; even a mundane breakfast was a riot. Just to clarify, the quality of the food was excellent, however, I am or will never ever be a man who enjoys having to eat before 11am. It does not seem normal. Still, watching Stomp charm the waitress and ingratiate himself with the rest of the hotel staff helped the food go down. It is hard to remember a better non-sexual start to the day.

After a cheery thanks to the breakfast staff our first appointment loomed large. It was now or never. Time to go to business. Despite all rumours to the contrary I do not tell that many lies. The odd white one, to a client, and that is that. Therefore, there is no need to raise Alfred Hitchcock from the dead to build the suspense at the bank. There were no sweaty palms, squeaky bums, or palpitations of the heart. The money was there, clean as a whistle. Ha. We both had sunshine in our smiles.

So much joy to come and brand new bright tomorrow awaited. We had only gone and done it. The clerks had no questions and just wanted instructions. Wunderbar, as our new Swiss friends heard us say. My role was IT, so I gave them some account information to fire the money to and Geert, of course, asked for some cash; he loved it, after all. He is a great guy but I guess this is his Achilles heel. In total he had asked for seven hundred one thousand Swiss Franc notes, eight hundred two hundred Franc notes, and a thousand hundred Franc notes. God bless the staff, they asked him if he wanted to make it up to a million in cash in fifties, twenties and tens. You bet your sweet bottom dollar he did. He pocketed 85% and gave me the rest, this time in a red velvet bag from the bank. Grinning from ear to ear, he asked me where next.

There was one more bank which before he asked I informed him would be purely electronic transactions only. Then to the Swiss equivalent of a chamber of commerce to register some companies and a meeting with an estate agent about a café that would be handy to start our property portfolio. All went as smoothly as the famed chocolate and we were just as rich by the end of the day. We made quite a team; guess he had the looks and I had the brain so we did make lots of money. It did not hurt, as like most Dutch people Geert spoke perfect German and for one day only I had used my best Hugh Grant accent. The term 'smoked' them came to mind as we had both the banking languages of the town down. The gnomes of Zurich were not adverse to our cash either, so things could not have gone better.

Sitting in the hotel bar after our triumphs, we debated what to do next. Mr Tromp wanted to fire up the next deal; after the thrill of the day it was hard to disagree but I managed to suggest a cooling-off period by quoting none other than Mr Desiderius Erasmus, saying that prevention was the best cure to any rash calls that could lead to mistakes. A seismic smile spread across his face followed by a firm handshake, a pat on the back, and a genuine hug of gratitude.

Ha. The rest of the world did not stand a chance. The night stretched out before us; though neither of us really drank, we both enjoyed being out and about. So we headed out to see what Zurich had to offer us. It is fair to say with cash on the hip we naturally headed up-market and spent an eye-watering amount on soft drinks and dinner. Still, it felt good to be sat at the top table. The barkeepers are real aficionados, happy to mix non-alcoholic cocktails and without wishing to appear a snob, there was an international elegance to most of the venues we frequented where there seems to be a long-forgotten world of style and grace. Oh, pleasant exercise of hope and joy!

However – big drum roll, or at least a cymbal tinkling – there was no bliss to be found at dawn.

One of the coolest men I have ever met was extremely agitated. Strange, to say the least. Blondie was pacing up and down the lobby; he barely acknowledged my wave and far more worryingly he did not even seem to notice the pretty receptionist. He was yammering into a mobile in what I can only assume was Dutch with maybe some Spanish thrown in as well, from what I overhead. Hum... Whatever could be the problem? I was reasonably sure it had nothing to do with our business so wandered into breakfast only mildly curious. I was just blowing the steam off my coffee when saw the gleam in the waitress's eye which though I am no Quasimodo, could only mean Geert was heading to the table. He did greet her, however with none of the flamboyance of the day before and so she slunk away slightly confused. The plot had thickened.

So should I say something or go? Well, they say the only way to know if you are really good friends with someone is to test the relationship. So, I drew breath and asked if everything was okay. He seemed quite taken off guard by this. He thanked me sincerely, then a handshake, then the trademark smile returned. Phew! Geert told me that he had some minor family problems that he was going to have to take care of and asked if it would be okay if I tied up the loose ends today. Sure, no problem. There was not that much on the agenda today anyway, we were just supposed to be looking over some high cash yield businesses such as cafés, a taxi firm, and a bar, though I was not that keen on the bar due to having to apply for a licence. Still worth a look.

We agreed to meet in the UK in two weeks' time where we could plan the next move. All seemed fine except there was something nagging away at me like a deranged spouse. Even though we were on great terms and there was trust and understanding, neither of us had ever talked to each other that much about family or relationships. I did not know if Geert was married, had children or any other meaningful relationship. He was often accompanied by a nubile young sex goddess and certainly had an eye for the ladies. On my side, he did not know much except I was married and quite pleased about it, as I had refused a couple of day-trippers from the Playboy mansion. The question was, was it important or not? Hard to say at this point, it was just a little odd but in a good way that he had put his family before business and pleasure.

When you deal with people who have money it is best not to judge and if you do have any morals it is best not to hand them out like business cards. You meet all sorts and in my humble opinion nobody is perfect. How could I possibly judge anyone? I had CHF150,000 in dubious cash in my room and a lot more in various accounts around the globe. As I said, nobody is perfect!

Maybe in attempt to match Mr Tromp's family-first philosophy, I thought, *What the hell? May as well give the missus a bell and get her over here for the weekend. Sure she would appreciate it.* I had told her I was due a bonus (just a white lie, honest) and as you will soon discover inconsistency is my very essence. She jumped at the chance and what a time it was, and in reference to an earlier point, sex is still the best way to start the day. A very agreeable weekend indeed.

At this point you may have some questions. Fair enough. Sure the first is were we not just recently informed that it is difficult to deposit large amounts of cash?

Yes.

Well what the fuck did you do with all the cash in the room?

No need to swear, though a very valid point. Try not to worry about it, for now let's just say it was sorted.

Secondly, was your wife not suspicious?

Of what?

The money, the last-minute trip, the luxury hotel, and your sudden wealth?

No.

Next, what about work? Thought you had a job, how can you just keep leaving the office?

This is easy to answer; investment bankers do not work by the clock and as long as you tell them you are chasing a deal, you can breeze in and out of the office as long as the cash keeps on coming.

Finally, why were you not more concerned about your business partner's sudden family problems?

Tricky. It just seemed genuine. Plus, not a biggy as no cash was involved that day. Happy?

Oh well, the best I can offer you at the moment is it is like when you watch a horror movie. From the outsider's view you would always ask yourself, why go into the dark creepy house? There is nor will there ever be an answer to this question. All you can say is, "Don't go in there. Don't go in there!"

So just close your eyes and try and show no surprise as I fail to change your mind.

CHAPTER 7

So close

An uneventful week back in Blighty was spent tending to my tedious clients' needs. It was getting harder to play the mild-mannered banker by day when I was a supervillain by night. Blimey, they suck the life out of you. In the past I had seen it as a necessary evil. Now though, with my access to cash, I had to do it through gritted teeth. Not yet, not yet. Still need them, the bank, the contact, just a couple more then no more. Hang in there, baby.

It would take someone with greater literary talents than me to describe investors' idiosyncrasies; words sadly fail me. Happily, there was a Cruyff turn to events when his biggest fan got in contact a week early. Just the ticket to help me evade and accelerate away from the tedium of the office.

Though the Dutch speak English very well, with an extensive vocab, it does not take Colombo to figure out they are not native speakers. The men sound like a drunk Sean Connery. "Hello Misster

Simon." Fair to say it was good to hear from my friend. He wanted to meet ASAP, which was fine by me. After another epic back-slapping session. Blimey, may have to take Jean Pierre up on his offer if this carries on.

Who?

Please keep up. French client of massage parlour, call girl fame.

We talked business. The G-men wanted, or more dramatically, needed to know how much cash-wise was possible to launder in one go. Even Stevie Wonder should have seen what was coming. Please feel free to replace Mr Wonder with Mr Magoo if you are a fan. Just wanted to colour the description a tad, we could always go with blind man if we must. Have to admit I was a little taken aback but before I was about to air any grievances Mr T. explained they had just received a huge payment from a government contract for building something or other. Even though they were the lowest bidder they were going to be paid well over the odds for the work. However, they had insisted on half in cash to avoid bank charges. The clincher was that the cash would allow them to pay contractors up front to get the job moving. Apparently a few local mayors were in their pocket as there was also a cashback offer under the table. In hindsight when you analyse this explanation it appears to be at the very least quite far-fetched. Or is it quite plausible? Please ask your local councillor and then look at their face as they deny it.

All of this meant the group were now swimming in gilders. In the past they had come up with some interesting ways of hiding and moving their money around. They had invented a tulip scam which wilted, given cash to couriers who got caught, and set up a coffee shop that went to pot. It was nice to be needed, but how much could I say to keep them happy while still avoiding detection? Tricky, tricky, tricky. We had done four deals so far totalling four million dollars, What the hell? Double trouble it is, so I suggested four. It would be possible even though it would not be easy for me, but clearly it was what Geert was looking for. Yet another back slap.

A far more appetising offer followed; as a thank you, dinner was offered at the Ivy. He also instructed me to bring my wife. Hmm – a silent 'why?' Sure this was picked up on. I was told, "It would be great to meet the woman who keeps you so honest."

It is said that a person who can bring laughter into a room cannot be all bad. The tonic water I was drinking came through my nose after this particular comment. Top man!

My wife had accompanied me to client dinners before, bless her, and had managed to fake interest in some desperately dull people. Pretty sure that was all she faked. Anyway, most of the time her presence, while not exactly under duress, I'm sure it did not figure in her list of things to do for an evening. In fairness it is not high on my priorities either. Having dinner with some boring business person would make a night in watching Big Brother seem preferable.

However, on this particular evening my wife was as giddy as a schoolgirl before a boyband concert. In spite of her many qualities she is a sucker for celebrities, whether it be in the magazines or on TV. Therefore, with the Ivy's reputation as a well-known hangout of the famous, she was ready to hot foot out before me. Thank heavens we were a few years from the selfie. I had planned to drive due to a ridiculous early meeting followed by a crappy client conference call. But just as I was searching for my keys there was a buzz on the intercom. If Mrs C. was not animated enough, she ran over, hugged and kissed me and screamed, "Limo!"

Thank God she did not pat my back. There was a suited and booted man waiting outside who informed me that my friend Frans had sent the car for Rembrandt. It would not be overdoing it to say my smile lit up the night. The ride to the restaurant was a merry one; the missus was beside herself and if it were not for the promise of a bit of celebrity watching, I'm not sure we would have made it. Still, it looked promising sex-wise for the immediate future.

On that front I was trying to exit the car with my dignity intact when the unmistakable tone of Geert boomed hello. As per usual, he was charm personified. The only thing missing was his trademark nubile pretty young minx. Instead he was accompanied by an extremely classy-looking lady whose age was hard to calculate, she looked a little older than me and Blondie but not by much. So I was a little a taken aback when she was introduced as his mother. Blimey, it is not an exaggeration to say that his mother could be his slightly older hot sister instead. After a little air kissing all round, we strolled towards the restaurant. Wouldn't you know it, we were even papped on the way in. My wife though, normally none too shabby in the class stakes, could hardly contain herself with all of this glamour, her usual air of cool disintegrating by the minute. According to my better half there were several A-list folk in the room, news to me. Still, anything that keeps her happy.

The meal was a merry one. My friend Frans erred on the side of caution on the charm stakes. Normally when there was a lady present he would be set to full-on flirt mode, however, there was just a soup song for my wife which I took as a sign of respect. Cheers, Dutchman. His mother was an absolute delight to be around. Not only a great conversationalist but a fascinating lady to boot. We all put the world to rights, laughed, joked, and the enjoyment peaked when another diner came to our table and told Frans he was great in The Hitcher and Blade Runner.

Our evening was complete when on leaving the owner came over and welcomed us to the Ivy Family. The place really does deserve its reputation as a great London dining institution.

Over a nightcap my wife asked Ma Tromp if she was staying longer as she must come to ours for dinner. Her reply was doubly delightful as one, she was going home the next day, and two, her super son had just brought her to London to cheer her up after a little family hiccup.

Marvellous though they were, and both great company, I desperately needed to start planning how to move the money around and would have no time as I had a full schedule day-job wise. The best part was that Geert did have some minor family problems. Ha, yaw boo sucks to the lot of you.

Even though my slightly tipsy wife was nibbling on

my ear in the limo, the problem of the money was oozing from my subconscious into my current focal awareness. It was hard to focus on the job in hand when my good lady's hot breath whispered, "Why don't we take a holiday? Give Gareth a call, let's go to Singapore and maybe Malaysia."

Fucking genius, Gareth has his own company there and has contacts all over Asia, Singapore, and Macau et al. Guess it is time to lie back and think of money. To avoid winning the bad sex fiction award let us consult Jane Austen and with a slight modification, say, 'It is a truth universally acknowledged, that a man in possession of a good fortune, must be in want of a wife.'

Before I drift off into a post-coital sleep, it's important that you know that Gareth will not be dragged into this. He is one of my oldest friends so I would never get him involved in anything illegal. His family and himself have been very good to me over the years. I feel better now – night to sleep and to dare to dream.

In the morning, I gave Gaz a call and asked if we could pop over as I needed a break.

"Course you can, mate."

Great. Remember, the trip is pleasure but I have to admit it will help as, while there, it would be simple to open a few accounts, check out some cash companies. Phoned Mrs C. – a few woops and a 'love you'. Oh dear. Far too busy at work to consult with my conscience, however, I did a few normal deals without really trying – strange. Guess it is not dissimilar to the attractiveness of happily married men to single women. They give off an air of confidence and the lack of interest, it seems like a powerful aphrodisiac. My clients seemed to be falling over themselves to consult me and more keen than ever to do business; my commission for the day was a personal record. Who would have thought that?

In the car on the way home I started calculating my cut so far plus my own legit savings and assets, and when it would be possible to leave both of my current worlds behind. When the next dodgy deal went through I would be ahead by 1.2 million dollars. I had put 100k back to the bank, which while annoying was a necessary evil. However, with salary and bonuses I would get that back and then some. So, with everything, that was around $1.5 million which made the magic one million pound mark. The question was, will that last a lifetime? To answer my own question, it would fund a reasonably comfortable life. Sadly, the goal was a good life, good life, life.

Before you start quibbling, I know, what an arsehole. Unfortunately for you, at the time no one else shared your current opinion. G and his men, work, Anne, my parents (more of them later), were all happy with me. Guess at the time I was pretty pleased with myself. What a bastard.

Well at least the promise of a trip to Singapore is forthcoming. It is also known as the Lion City, Garden City, and bizarrely the Red Dot. Therefore, if you are looking for ideas for a future trip, what follows may sell Singapore.

Before we set off, a quick word. Better quickly explain how we get the all-clear from the office and sell Anne on the idea of the need for me to disappear for a couple of half days first. It would have been easy to just put in a holiday request as I was owed some, however, I was still a little annoyed about putting money in to the bank to keep my cover. So fuck it. Told them it is a business trip. Magic – flights paid, expenses, and even wangled my wife's flight as I claimed to be saving them money by staying with a friend. With the extortionate cost of a reasonable room in Singapore it was an extremely easy sell. Man, am I on fire or what? Smoking. Please feel free to scroll up for your previous opinion to help save your breath. The flight to Singapore is now boarding. The destination had once just been considered a sterile stopover on the way to Australia. Cannot remember the guy's name so please do not sue; it was once described as Disneyland with the death penalty.

Not anymore. Though they still have the death penalty and you cannot drop litter, it has transformed into a must-see city. Many a hippie may disagree but who listens to them? However, to most it is a welcome respite from the dirt, chaos, crime, and dare I say poverty of much of the Southeast Asian mainland. The following is all on offer in an area easy to get around. For your entertainment you have beaches – clean, tropical, and uncluttered, super tax-free shopping if that is your thing, history and museums – all in English, my monolingual chums. Nature and wildlife is everywhere, with night safari, botanical gardens, and the Bukit Tinama reserve has more plant species than North America. If memory serves me right, I think you can feed tortoises and turtles somewhere. You have the town of yesteryear blending into the ultra-modern city, parks, and the Garden City is in fact a garden. Throw in fab food which is legendary and an ever-improving nightlife. What more do you want? If this were a post card we can say 'wish you were here'. Especially as the rain falls down on your humdrum town. Just call me Judith. Not bad, is it, three trips and three wins? This run of fortune will come to an end for the benefit of those with a schadenfreude nature. Rome, for instance, is up there with finding out that Santa Claus is not real as one of the greatest disappointments of my life.

Back to better climes. The sun was out, I had a cool drink in my hand and was watching my good lady and Gareth's latest muse splashing around in the pool. Ah, the good life. I had forgotten with all the recent activity that my last break was over six months ago and that I really needed a rest. So the first few days were business free and concentrated on recharging my batteries.

It had been a while since myself and Gareth had managed to meet up so it was just fun to pick up where we left off. We had a mutual understanding and could just talk utter crap and of course take the piss out of each other. We also had a long-running wager on everything from a round of golf to a game of pool and would even bet on how long we could each hold a burning match. Not sure who was ahead so it must have been Gaz. Be prepared to have your trust stretched to the very edges. As we shot the breeze my friend mentioned that there was a business dinner he had to go to and asked if we would come along.

Guess what? There were various companies who needed banking advice in Europe and there would be other leading lights from the financial world present. Hard as this is to swallow, please suspend your disbelief and join us in the long bar at Raffles Hotel,

Singapore. Slings on me. If you would like a complex review please read Somerset Maugham; his thoughts are worth the room rate. While you are at it check out his short stories – a true wordsmith at work.

If you are tired of the business talk and just want to enjoy your drink, that is perfectly understandable. For the record, let me draw your attention to the Singapore government's own advice to foreign investors. 'In our country you can set up a new business in a matter of hours.' No wonder the World Bank rank it as the easiest place to operate. Cheers. Another. Needless to say all went to plan – deals done, real and irregular – then got to enjoy a great break. If you would like a full run-down of all the transactions completed and how the money was hid, please feel free to consult the 'con artists are us' reference in the back.

Even though I have and would continue to roam the world, those were the days to breathe, to dream and feel the sun on my back. Those were the days indeed. For those waiting around the corner with the bad news, lucky you.

After foolishly checking my e-mail, there was a message from Geert. I opened it tentatively and sure enough he and all his associates would last a day. Even though I was sure it would just be a pat on my poor back. I much preferred the idea of the G-men as a non-existent necessity for my retirement plans. I enjoyed my time with Blondie but I was just happy to hear about his partner's happiness. Shit. Remember the tip about business class for less than three hours? Good. Well if you do have to go further, save up, or get the company to pay, or beg the desk for an upgrade as it is a must for long haul. Thankfully, due to my recent run of success the bank had paid for mine. All of this is a long-haul, and thanks to the comfort my wife was soundly asleep on the way home. This allowed me the time to think.

How many more? The last few days basking around Gareth's pool and sampling superb Singapore had blotted any wrongdoing from my brain; the good life was the goal. At the moment I had enough for the not-bad life – that was not enough. Sorry, it sounds crass but better to aim high to have a champagne life; you cannot do it on a beer budget. Managed a fitful sleep. How many more? For the devils in the detail out there, we gave Malaysia a miss.

Amanda (Gareth's model girlfriend) convinced us by describing it as earthy and real. This is not a slight as I'm all for that but as she said, "Malaysia is for smelly hippies."

For anyone reading from the tourist board, we will drop in on Kuala Lumpur later. Back in the office, the palms were out, the smiles were beaming; the deals had been rolling in from Asia. It is fair to say had earned my air fare. Therefore, as it was all good on the real work front I gave Blondie a bell. He was his usual jovial self and heaven knows how he knew about my nervousness about the meeting, but he did. Anticipation was a skill of his; he insisted the meeting take place in London, good, and it was just a thank you meeting. Ok then. The Dorchester was offered up. Guess I could slum it there for the evening. Except it was not an evening meeting.

CHAPTER 8

It is not what you think

The first surprise for my first formal introduction to the G-men was that they wanted to meet for afternoon tea. Strange thing about the Dutch, they come over all casual and laid back. However, they do like a little elegance and opulence. Geert explained that after reading the dress code he had to go. The hotel respectfully asks guests to refrain from wearing baseball caps, beanie hats, ripped jeans, sportswear, trainers, flip-flops, and shorts. Please dress to impress. "I love you crazy fucking English and your rigid rules." Marvellous.

On the dress front my father had drummed into me from an early age of not running with the pack and always dressing in style. You would think this would have been a difficult thing to do as a teenager. Nah, for those with memories of the late eighties, not difficult at all. Some may say the suit is out – they are wrong. Look back at pictures of people in the 50s and 60s – they looked great. Somewhere after that, people stopped dressing. Designer sportswear, NO

THANKS! Here endeth the lesson.

The second surprise was watching Geert and his so-called G-men nibbling on cucumber sandwiches when I arrived at the Promenade. Surely men who take afternoon tea cannot be all that bad. Frans jumped up on my arrival, easy fellow. The welcome was sincere, however. He then started the introductions. There was Vinny (Van Gogh), Hieo (Bosch) and Jan (Vermeer). As well as calling themselves G-men they saw themselves as artists, so all greeted me as Rembrandt. Who knew or cared what their names were/are? Like the setting the company was gracious and charming. There was nothing but praise for my efforts and like Geert, Frans for now, all were great company. Business was not on the table which was a good job as the table was overflowing. There were savoury finger sandwiches; fillings included smoked salmon, chicken, prawn, and of course the fabled cucumber. If this were not enough, scones, cakes, tartlets, and the pièce de résistance of a praline pyramid festooned the table. My cup was also overflowing with tea and the milk of Dutch kindness.

Our table was a merry one and made more so when our resident artists drew me a picture of their previous failed cleaning attempts. None of them had shined and it was hugely entertaining listening to the ribbing they gave each other. Guess we can say this was surprise number three, as the British tend to think they have the market corned in piss-taking. Well that may or may not be true, but better watch out – the Dutch are a close second if there is a competition. It is hard to say who had made the biggest cock-up.

My own personal favourite was Jan's crackpot tulip ruse. The idea was to pour cash into fields and fields of tulips. Then when the flowers were sold around Europe the money would be as sweet smelling as its namesake.

The only blip was Jan knew nothing about plants and weather. In an attempt to get the product to the market ahead of the competition he had miscalculated the length of the winter in Holland. Bloody berk. His companions called him Piet Oudolf. Nah, me neither. He is a well-known garden designer from the Netherlands apparently. Anyway, we all laughed the afternoon away. What good company; these men cannot be bad guys, they have style, taste, and are a great laugh.

Tea had been drunk all afternoon, however, Vinny ordered champagne and proposed a toast. "To the dream and Mr Rembrandt, our cash mastermind." A little embarrassing but what the hell? Cheers.

On the way out Geert asked for a quick word. He smiled that Blondie smile and handed me a striking leather briefcase. He told me he and his men could not thank me enough and the case and what was inside was a recognition of the work I had done. "Simon, my friend, I knew you were our guy, so we feel a bonus is in order." See you in a month.

It appears he was no longer looking for special kind of business partner. I was his guy. What was a man to do? What indeed? In fact, there was more than a minor bonus. Inside the case was £100,000 in cold hard cash. Told you, criminals cannot get enough of the stuff. The look on their faces when they have it is amazing. Forget women, food, cars, pools, houses, and every other luxury. Money is magic to them. Hence, if they like you they share the love. Sure, most of you would love to have a briefcase full of money. If you could smell or touch the case, pretty sure that you would consider it a wonderful present.

Now if previous form is anything to go on, you would be expecting a load of bleating and moaning, a dab of 'woe is me' and some other self-obsessed 'what is a man to do?' nonsense. Ha. Not a bit of it. Pack it up, pack it in, let me begin by saying I came to win and now may be a good time to jump around. Think you may know the rest. Ok then. Jump up, jump up and get down. Remember, inconsistency is the only constant on sale here, unless we go back to the previous advice of not putting your money under a mattress. Remember, banks hate you but are slightly safer. The last few confusing words are a way of saying that if you have 100k in cash the safest place to put it is in a bank. So, following my own advice I popped backed to the office and after taking about three grand out, left the case in my office in my own personal locked cabinet. Genius or madness – you decide.

The case for genius. The office where I work is extremely difficult to get into for staff, let alone anyone else. Also better to hide things in plain sight than under a bed, and I can take cash out over the coming weeks and months and in the process I'm not spending clean money. The case for madness. What idiot would leave that amount of money in an office? As the self-appointed returning office, still think it is fucking genius. At this point I have to sign off today as I have some social functions to perform.

Two friends who have supported me through thick

and thin are in town so I will be spending time with them. Do not fret, as I have the next three days free to break the back of this book. I think we are between 25-35 percent done. Is everyone okay? Hope so.

Let us continue with the money in my office. I opened a few savings accounts, paid off all my bills in cash, cleared my wife's credit cards, and even gave my brother some cash – well, helped the heart. The legal money continued to roll in and it got to the point where I would have to advise myself. Life is but a dream at this point. The only thing that was worrying me at this point was how much I was looking forward to the next deal. Blondie had been in touch a couple of times and we had even been to a film premier together. My wife was obviously over the moon with this development.

The month slowly drew to an end, with the day job routine biting hard. Finally, we were there. The big Dutch man was back in town and it was my turn to be like a giddy teenager waiting for their first gig. Not sure what the British or Holland equivalent is of bros but that's what we were to each other now. Bezzies, mates, vriendschap, chums, or just prefer good friends. We met at a quiet, nondescript coffee shop. Laughter was served first followed by a quick catch-up, then it was down to business. As always in these situations the attractive, disinterested, trendy waitress who had come over at below zero to me, was warming by the second to our man. It was hard to suppress a smile until she called me on it, how rude. Explained we were gay lovers and she had less than no chance. Ha, take that, you surly cow. This added to our earlier amusement and delayed what we had met for. This hardly seemed to matter.

With the waitress finally out of earshot, Geert began. He started by explaining that they had hidden a large amount of cash from all the dodgy white-collar crime in an old warehouse in Holland. The G-men had popped in from time to time to make withdrawals yet the piles of cash still remained as high as ever. To get to the point, they wanted to sell the property to a local developer so needed the cash out. All seemed to be in order so I just asked how much? Of course he did not know, a shrug which was followed by a wink and the famed smile. Guess another trip to Clog Land was in order to find out.

On the way out Blondie took my hand and then blew our now sour server a kiss and said she was welcome to come and watch. What a guy!

We spent the rest of the afternoon in Fortnum and Masons over a fifty quid cup of tea. Cor blimey, guvnor, as they say in these parts. In respect to fine establishment, they do throw in the odd cake or two with the tea. We also managed to attract the attention of the blue rinse brigade, who informed Blondie he could make an even bigger fortune as a toy boy. Another blinding day.

CHAPTER 9

One more deal should do it

Work-wise and relationship-wise was double good, so another trip would not raise a single eyebrow. To make sure, I scheduled in a trip to see JP in France as well. Apart from the odd dalliance away from his loving wife, Jean was hard to fault. Besides, he informed me that he was given a mistress as a wedding present. Unlike most clients, you got what you saw and he was good to hang around with. Business-wise, he was as sharp as the suits he wore. You never left a meeting with him without picking up a useful stock tip or getting wind of a merger or takeover. He usually threw in an excellent dinner too. I decided to drive as it would allow me time to think and believed it would keep me off the radar metaphorically and literally. Though, I'm sure we have done that before. Crap, I've just told you there were no raised eyebrows. Well, it is fair to say that my decision to drive may have met with the odd arch or two. To compensate for this, I had prepared a retort to the misgiving raised.

The missus fell for this 'would be a chance to load up on wine' line. I did also honestly say that after our recent trip I was not as motivated at work and needed a longer break from the daily grind. I threw in my sleepy, sad puppy eyes and earned a huge hug a kiss and a 'take your time' line. You go, girl. Thanks Anne. Oh, those hugs. That one was more or less deserved as I genuinely did need to get away from the office as the monotony was getting to me. It was hard to sit in soulless conference rooms and look at spreadsheets and complete reports with a million in the bank. It was not enough. I know, I know. Still, it was not enough. So I sucked it up, gritted my teeth, and came up with some crap to explain the car to work. They went for the need to meet clients in various places and of course the financial savings offered up. This was again closer to the truth than you may care to believe. For a start, I had agreed to meet Jean Pierre in Deauville (in Normandy) so it was easier to drive. My PA had got one of those cheap ferry deals so saving the bank paying way over the odds for business class to Paris. See? If you are going to lie, tell the truth first. What my assistant had failed to let me know was that my trip included an overnight in Le Havre. This was completely financially based, my own stupid fault as I had asked her to find the skin flint deal.

The last ferry of the day was booked which arrived at stupid o'clock and Bates Motel in LH was pre-booked for a few hours' sleep, and with a soggy croissant for free. It was obviously not called Bates Motel – that would have been an upgrade. I believe it was part of the Formula 1 chain. The shower and the toilet are in a pod which turns into a human car wash. There are no staff, no freebies, cold coffee, and the above-mentioned day-old pastry. Speaking of toilets, that would be my best review of Le Havre. It is only famous for one reason: unlike Paris, it was heavily bombed in the Second World War.

Then a chap named Auguste Perret decided to rebuild the city in just concrete. Any colour you want as long as it was grey. There was an oil, chemical, and automotive industries boom after the war but the 1970s marked the end of that and the beginning of the economic crisis: the population declined, unemployment increased and remains at a high level today. To get to the point, the place is a shit hole. I drove away from my hotel as fast as my car would take me.

Thankfully it was pre speed camera days. Thank heavens then for Deauville. This was my real port – or beach if you prefer – of call. Ah, what a difference 43hm makes – just a forty-minute drive. Nestled into the resort of Côte Fleurie of France's Lower Normandy region, the resort is known for its grand casino, golf courses, horse races, and wide sandy beach. The beach is backed by Les Planches, a 1920s boardwalk with bathing cabins. The town has chic written all over it with elegant belle epoque villas and half-timbered buildings. Breathe in that fresh sea air, and watch the sun start to light up the clean white beaches and bounce on the water – magic.

Hope this is not blasphemy but morning had broken, sunlight from heaven, mine was the sunlight, mine was the morning. Praise indeed for the morning. I am tired both then and now so please accept this copy and paste from Amsterdam. Having arrived early I spent the morning just people watching, something that never seems to lose its appeal, especially in foreign climes. There is also a pleasant feeling of anonymity when you are in another country. The town's glamour has remained intact and I had parked myself in the Bar de la Mer, where it's easy to picture devotees of the past, such as Coco Chanel or Colette, and spent the time admiring the stylish locals park their elegant butts in their LBDs in the famed café chairs. See? We may have only travelled a short distance geographically, however, we are light years away in terms of culture and style.

The place is famed for several reasons, from the film 'Un Homme et Une Femme', which forever connected the town to romance and to its theme tune, *Chabadabada*. In France, it is known perhaps above all for its role in Marcel Proust's 'In Search of Lost Time', also translated as 'Remembrance of Things Past'. To the rest of us, James Bond gambled with the Russians in the casino and Tom and Daisy honeymooned in from the Great Gatsby, not half bad. I expect a cheque from the locals any day now.

Let us drag ourselves away and back to heavenly morning. The peace and quiet was pierced with a booming bonjour from JP. People in my world are almost bipolar because of the two different microscopes they are under. In the office, at conferences, meetings, and day-to-day, they are conservative with a capital C, studiously examining spreadsheets and speaking in reverent tones to important clients and superiors. Once they manage to escape the confines of this office prison the fresh air can get to them... Jean was like a Labrador running around the café; he greeted me, ran over to check the view, breathed in the air, checked out the ladies, smiled at the waitress and eventually sat down. The ego had landed. Therein lies the rub. Outside the office people like JP and my other clients and colleagues are expected to be oozing in self-confidence bordering on arrogance. You get used to it and learn to live with it. I knew for a fact Jean Pierre had been locked away working on a takeover for months. Clearly he spoke machine-gun style French to me. Lentement, s'il vous plait. Sorry, I am trying to appear multilingual. In the interests of full disclosure my French is passable, which is why the bank gave me all their French business. Pas de problème pour moi, pardon.

I ordered tea, as this was a man who obviously did not need coffee. He was as well-groomed as always and I guess he was not dissimilar in looks to the French actor in 'Betty Blues', whose name escapes me for now. Betty was portrayed by Beatrice Dalle, it will come to me. Anyway, after he caught his breath and returned to speaking at normal speed he filled me in on the plan for the day. We were booked into the Hotel Royal Barriere which was comped by the group backing the takeover, happy days for the office. None too shabby for me either. The plan was lunch, the races, dinner, and the casino at some point. We might even get round to business but there was no rush. To borrow another Amsterdam phrase, had worse days. Jean. Ah, that is it. Jean was the actor's name. Jean Anglade. Few can enjoy the day. To avoid repetition, my friend JP was thrilled with the plan; he even pointed out that even if we lost in the casino we could not lose in any other way. How right he was. I logged numerous sure-thing stock tips and was given the inside track on the newly unannounced merger. Some may say this is insider trading, that cannot be true when you are in amazing surroundings and it is catered.

The best news was that I met several companies that were looking for cash investment no questions asked. Even better was that one guy fitted the G-men profile and his company was based in Reims, slap bang in the champagne region of France. Cheers, everyone. In the casino Jean wandered over with two young Bridgette Bardot lookalikes linking his arms. No wonder he could not take the smile off his face. He managed to untangle himself from Anne and Marie to embrace me, full-on French-style kisses included. My obvious discomfort amused the ladies immensely, however, after I had wrestled free from my French friend the ladies began hugging and kissing me. While this was certainly not an unpleasant experience with one even singing 'Lady Marmalade' in my ear, to tell the truth this was the most tempted I had ever been. This seemed to spur the lady on to inspect my ear with her tongue. Good job I cleaned the blighter.

Thankfully I realised that I was putting one part of my life at risk, so why fuck up the rest for a fuck? After agreeing to meet JP in the morning, to coin an old Fleet Street phrase I made my excuses and left. The only thing of note the following day apart from another gorgeous sun-drenched day, was Jean Pierre's attire. He was still in last night's dinner get-up, though slightly more dishevelled. Still cool as, mind. The business had all been done the day before therefore I just watched on in interest as my client tried to force a pastry down. Strange as it may seem, once again I had done a fair amount of deals the day before had even put the office on to the take-over, which was received with joy and glad tidings. More good news, after his evening of horizontal jogging with one or both of the Bardots, Jean Pierre was pooped. This meant that he could not get out of his chair to bid me adieu, and slobber on me again. I got a huge smile and with unrecognised irony, patted him on the back. Au revoir, mate. Thanks for a great day. The great day was well and truly true. As well as the above, I had bagged an appointment today in Reims. Hands up, who wants more details of this? Good, neither did Geert; he just told me to keep doing what I was doing. Even though you did not put up your hand your suspicion may have been roused about the lack of detail. There is a good reason for this and as we have not had a multiple choice for a while, let us drive down that avenue once more.

The business to which we are referring is so extremely complicated and diverse that it would take forever and a day to go into detail. It is very difficult to remember the exact details. The gentlemen who run the company would not like it. Blondie and me may or may not still have some cash there.

Shame we get to miss the joie de vivre of Reims. Well, take a weekend break if you get the chance. It is one of France's most intriguing small urban pockets, a place of culinary flair, rich medieval history, and exotic Art Deco architecture. Instead we get to stand in a warehouse looking at walls and walls of cash.

CHAPTER 10

Is this the end?

I was just south of Eindhoven in the Netherlands. I had tickled the G-men by giving the each a chip from the casino in Deauville. Vinny was still laughing like a good one as I tried to take in the enormity of the task in hand. Jan, while still grinning, spinning his chip, asked what we should do. It was amazing that their love of cash seemed to limit common sense. The first part was easy, I had seen the chaos coming and had brought several cash counters with me. Another valid point for coming in the car. Sorry, forgot to mention that to anyone. One thing that cheered me up was that there was just the five of us. No outsiders, always follow the mantra of what cannot speak cannot lie. The downside was that we would have to do all the counting. The money was 70/30 between Dutch guilders and US dollars. Though it was odd they had so many dollars, the main problem was the exchange rate. At the time, you got 2.5 guilders to 1 US dollar. That's why there was so much damn paper around us. More advice: if you are going to take on this particular odious task, do not wear an expensive suit.

My associates and I had failed to heed this and though I liked to think we looked good at the beginning of the day, that was not the case now. Still, the encouraging aspect was the hope this may lessen the G-men's love of cash. After all, hope springs eternal. The cash is weighed in; cash is weighed in from Eindhoven. Would you like it in dollars or pounds?

Going on the less is more mode, there was over eleven million quid – gulp. In order to get the best possible deal on the warehouse sale we had just over a month. Two thoughts. First, double your money try to get rich. Second, these latest events did unnerve me. Even though the wheels are turning, this amount is a very different story.

The others had started putting the bundles into boxes and looked over to me as to why I was not helping. I informed them that manual labour was not part of the deal. This brought tension-lifting laughter. Believe Jans may have wiped a tear away when informed that when I applied for the post of international money transferrer there was nothing in my contract about heavy lifting.

"Nice one, Rembrandt," was chorused, echoing around the warehouse.

As unofficial leader, Blondie decided this task was too demeaning for him as well. He suggested we take in some air. One of the many things that I really liked about him was his anticipation of my misgivings and problems. He apologised for the surroundings and the amount, then reassured me that we could take longer than a month as they had other property. Cheers. How did he manage to always placate me? Unlike the wife there was no sex; guilt trips worked for parents and siblings. Who knows? As we sat down outside two things settled my nerves completely. For one, Geert insisted on a pay rise to 20% plus bonus – cha-ching. Then heard a duck quack and I noticed a canal. Can you see the light bulb? A man, a plan, a canal. Panama. Bloody brilliant. The plan was as follows:

We could filter some money through France, siphon some to Singapore, launder some through Luxembourg and Liechtenstein, send some to Switzerland, then put the rest in Panama. Try to put well in practice what you already know, and in so doing, you will in good time, discover the hidden things which you now inquire about. Practice what you know, and it will help to make clear what now you do not know. In my defence, I guess all I can say is like Mr Rembrandt, a painting is only finished when the artists says so. Still in the game then, Blondie saw me smile and sensed I was okay. He did not even ask; he knew there was a plan.

The others joined, looking more like workmen than businessmen; they seem to be expecting some sort of gratitude. Not a bit of it. Geert started ripping into them and as I was in a far better mood I piled in behind him. To their credit, they laughed it off. My own personal favourite was the comparison between HB and his namesake Hieronymus Bosch's work. He did look like hell that is, for sure. After a clean-up, as well-deserved payback they made me eat raw herring which is some sort of Dutch delicacy – yuk. My reaction cheered the G-men no end. Well, they do say revenge is a dish best served cold. Told you these guys are great to be around. They can take a joke plus give it back. Geert, like Cruyff, is the mastermind. However, Jan, Vinny, and H as I now called him, all brought something to the party. We were all well and truly bonded. Handy in a warehouse.

The first four million was moved within the first month through the previous channels that had been set up. We all took a trip en masse to Zurich to spend some and jolly it up. I had also set up accounts in Singapore for all of them and was now working on France and Panama. At the beginning of the next month I had managed to move two million to Asia, with a further million plus to be deposited over the next month. The French company were very happy too, with a promise of cash investment of over one million, and gave us a 40% of the business. The next bit of trickery involved numerous accounts being zapped all over until the cash ended up in Panama. On paper this sounds quite easy. It wasn't – trust me. There were several sleepless nights, stabbing pains of conscience, and quite a bit of back and forth travel-wise. My good lady took it with her usual good grace and the office just saw the pound signs getting bigger.

After two months or more the deed was done – cash cleaned, Blondie and the boys blissfully happy, and I had over £3.5 million in Swiss bank accounts. In the office I was nailed on to be investor of the year and promotion was offered. It also meant a full bonus of over a year's salary. Retirement beckoned. Wish this was the happy end, my friends. Let us end the suspense once and for all – it was not the end. It should have been, it could have been, it wasn't. In fact, we are only at the beginning. I felt some suspense was necessary.

Mr Tromp had disappeared and the rest had all gone to ground. This was good news in a way as we had all agreed on a cooling-off period the last time we were all together. After the last two turbulent months everyone needed some respite. There was no time limit given and Blondie had told me in private that maybe the work is done. He of course did this in his inevitable style and in a very gracious way, and informed me that it might be time to get out. His argument was that we had been blessed with amazing luck and good timing. The money was safe and we all had enough for a good life. It was a compelling argument and I had to agree.

He then spoke to us all and said it had been an exciting ride, but quoting Mr Erasmus while smiling at me, said that prevention is better than cure, so why push our luck? So we unanimously agreed to a break. The G-men were delighted with my work; we were all friends with a fortune.

The autumn before the winter had been our last mad surge of youth. By Christmas when all my assists had been calculated plus the big B-day in January, I would have close to four million big ones. With the extra cash I had been given I had almost paid off my house, and stock tips for Mr Broker so I could rent or sell, so no expenses either. Enough. Christmas promised to be a merry one. The only hiccup was how to tell Anne and the bank that I wanted out. Maybe I could ask for a career break of six months just in case. That should do the trick. My boss and the office could wait until the New Year – to be exact, the day after the bonus hit my account. Mrs C. was the one to convince. When and where? Better before, so I decided on the Friday before the festivities got into full swing.

It was the office party which may appeal to some but was not my thing. Anne, though not the jealous type was happy that I was giving it a miss to take her out on the town. After a very agreeable dinner I told her was tired; she informed me she was too full for sex so not to worry. That was not quite the response I was expecting. Still, it actually helped. I drew breath and repeated the same line, this time adding 'with work' to the sentence. What do you know, my Anne, my wife, my love, held my hand, smiled, and told me to take a break. Ah, all is calm, all is bright.

So Christmas was indeed a merry one. Cheers everyone. Believe our American cousins would wish you a happy holiday.

It's a new year so the possibility of a new dawn and a new life hoping for something new.

Oh, the drama, just trying to avoid hitting the writer's wall.

Buoyed by a great Christmas and the prospect of the dream becoming reality, meeting my boss to ask for a break seemed less traumatic. Most people in my line of work question themselves from time to time, however, few leave the magnet of money drawing them back time after time. Luckily for me there was a way out of the daily grind.

After checking to see that my bonus had landed I made my way to my boss's grandiose office. The big man's secretary buzzed me in without checking for an appointment. After all, I may be the heir apparent. The chief was in a very good mood so it was clear he had also checked his bonus had gone in, so it could be a good day for bad news. As it had already worked once I tried the tired line again. Pretty sure he would not give my wife's initial answer. He didn't. We worked our way through the five stages of grief. There was denial, anger, bargaining, depression was replaced with anger again, then finally after a marathon meeting – acceptance.

The above are apparently used as part of the framework that makes up our learning to live with the one we lost. It seems the bank needed me and my boss's bonus had been raised due in some part to my efforts. Guess the strangest thing was his loss of composure and his willingness to show his hand so quickly. All good to know. As a compromise on my part, I agreed to just a three-month sabbatical, knowing full well if all went to plan that would be that. Of course the meeting **was not quite the end**. There were some loose ends to be tied. Clients had to be informed and a reason had to be agreed for PR purposes; it seemed that there were some family issues that I had to attend to in Australia, strewth!

The boss of bosses even stepped in, aka the CEO – praise indeed. He gave me some guff, telling me that employers' attitudes had changed as they realised that, in order to retain good employees, they may have to release them for a certain period of time. The organisation may benefit from an employee who returns with new skills, such as a new language or a professional qualification. In addition, the employee is likely to have a renewed and refreshed attitude to work. He stifled a smile then spoke off the record and praised my decision, telling me that I was on his list of the ones to watch and on my return fame and fortune was mine for the taking. What utter crap. Yet still, it was still good to hear. To cap the lot though, he took me to lunch and the very big B even asked me to walk alongside him through the office, in his words to piss off everyone else. Fair to say, I liked him and in other circumstances it would have been fun to hang around to see if I was indeed one to watch.

Sadly, that was the only positive part of the whole leaving process, where once I could float in and out and had carte blanche in my deals, my every move seemed to be monitored. Think they just wanted to make sure that I was not feeding anything to the dreaded completion. If only they knew the real reason. The days got longer and my work life was suffocating. It did not seem fair. My wife had her request for a break approved within seconds. She was told she deserved it and to have a great time. Finally, the slowest few weeks of my life drew to a close, all that remained was a drinks do. The main surprise after dreading it, was that it was actually a pleasant occasion. My boss even came along, got wildly drunk and praised me to the skies in his speech, hugged and kissed me, told me to hurry back, and then threw up in the toilets. What was not to like? Then that was that.

CHAPTER 11

The dream, the life

Do you know the way to San Francisco, or was it San Jose? It is not that important because San Francisco is where we are heading. It was the 1st of February, it was over 70 degrees, we had hired a brand-new convertible, and the world was ours. The sun was out, the wind was just right, and the city was on the horizon. The dream starts here.

We walked along the Golden Gate Bridge and were scared on the night tour of Alcatraz which I highly recommend. Ate fresh seafood, authentic Chinese, had a drink at the Mad Dog in the Fog where ex-pats are us. Cavorted in the Castro and all in all had a great time, then it was time to hit the road. The route chosen was not the most original; in fact it could be said to be the road most travelled in people's minds. The Pacific Highway is one of Americas most scenic and famous drives. It starts at the Northwest tip of the USA, running almost all the way to the Mexican border. Anne and myself had cheated by giving the north part a miss. Still, a feast of the senses awaited along with spiffy little seaside towns and curvy roads hugging huge stretches of the coast. The narrow road ribbons above the ocean, overlooking beaches cast like pearls, did not disappoint. Monterey Bay was mesmerising, the unspoilt coast line seemingly without end.

Time to get off the horse and drink some milk. Shit, that is John Wayne. If you are a little confused, let's clear that up. I know what you are thinking. Did we drive 80 miles or over 100 miles? Well, to tell you the truth, in all the excitement, as Anne was driving no one kept track. But being as we are in Carmel hopefully all is clear. Dirty Harry burgers were ordered, if that helps. No? Okay, the town is just after the bay and though the tourist authority may plug its natural scenery and rich artistic history, with 60 percent of Carmel's houses being built by citizens who were "devoting their lives to work connected to the aesthetic arts", it is most famous for appointing the man with no name as mayor. Still no idea? In 1986 Clint Eastwood was elected to govern the small wealthy town. He had certainly cleaned the place up – it was spotless. The burgers were not bad either.

Next on the tick list was Big Sur. Many people have waxed lyrical, extolling the raw beauty of the craggy unspoilt coastline. You had better believe them, the place is other worldly. Dream on. Believe Mr Disney said, "If you can dream it, do it." Cheers, Walt.

A few Santas followed – Maria and Barbara, with the latter sometimes described as the American Rivera due to the Mediterranean climate. Sure, in high season it could be a nightmare, however, as Anne and I rolled into town with the cool wind in our hair you could not complain. This was the life; I had not broached the subject of making it permanent to Mrs C. yet but seeing her revel in our new freedom and surroundings, I felt it would be less of a problem than before.

There was no rush though. There was wine to taste, huge portions of food to eat, and time to take in the Ocean. Bliss.

The City of Angels was next and at my request we drove in with 'LA Women' at full blast. Just a few words, please. We got into town about an hour ago, and took a look around to see which way the wind blew. Are you lucky little lady in the city of night, or just a lost angel? My angel smiled despite herself. Sure you do not need a tour of the town. Spoiler alert – in reality LA is a little disappointing because it is too frigging big. Still, there is plenty to do if you can ignore the traffic and distances involved getting from A to B. We could not ignore it and after a few smog-filled traffic jams sailed off to Catalina Island to get some fresh air and visit Avalon. Much better.

After another day back in LA just to shop we hit the highway and headed south towards San Diego. Los Angeles' sprawling metropolis aside, the trip had more than lived up to expectations. The blue sky was back and all was well so I casually dropped that wouldn't it be great to do this for the rest of time? Anne agreed. Getting easier by the day. Like most couples we had our ups and downs, however, the last few weeks of freedom had been some of the best in our relationship. I did not want them to end and nor should they. Come on, let the good times roll.

Talking about good times, imagine 70 miles of sun-drenched coast, an inviting ocean, and a year-round daily forecast of 70°F, and you'll understand why San Diego was the next port of call. Do you feel the need for speed? Me neither, however, it is also a deep-water port and home to Miramar of 'Top Gun' fame. That film seems so long ago, better to give it a miss and move on to steak. Well, the smell of it being cooked anyway. It wafts invitingly into the San Diego air. It must be a conspiracy to ensure that you do not order anything else. If it is, well, it worked on us. I sat sated to say the least, having just ate half a cow, washing it down with a cheeky little red. The missus even revoked her non-smoking policy to help further aid the digestion. Anne was smoking a menthol cigarette and I was trying to puff my way on a fine cigar. Ah, the good life. Between her failed attempts at smoke ring she said, "Let's never go back." The good life was there to be free and explore the unknown.

Like a telegraphed pass, rain on a bank holiday, you can probably see what is coming a mile away. If you will forgive me I would prefer not to broach the elephant in the room for a few more lines. Come with me just a short while, feel the warm balmy evening air. The satisfaction of a full stomach, the sound of the ocean lapping in the background. Swirl your wine in your glass, drink a little, then the person you love squeezes your hand and you get lost in their eyes. You have money to burn, zero responsibilities, and all the time in the world. Throw in a barefoot walk on the sand the smoothest creamiest ice cream you could wish for, and hopefully you can see my reluctance to move on from this moment.

CHAPTER 12

Carmen Camila Lopez

Fuck it, here goes. The start of the remorse and sadness and still trying to remember a lost love and lost life. With all the things that I said, I am still haunted by you in every town and every place.

We had tried to make the trip as tech-free as possible. It was pre-iPhone days, however, e-mail was all the rage. Though computers had been available in all the hotels on the route we had given them a wide berth. The only thing between us and the real world was a mobile phone the bank had left for me at San Francisco airport. Remember, it was not an iPhone, all it did, kids, was text and call. Before we find out why the bank left me a US mobile phone, please live your life – stop videoing it, taking pictures of it and like the poem, what is life if, full of care. We have no time to stand and stare. Get off your phones please, all of you.

Anyway, the phone was left just in case the bank needed anything, my stipulation being emergencies only. In fairness, it was free and it could be used for personal, so I had left the number on mine and Anne's phone's voicemail and had given the number to the usual suspects. We had both called the folks back home a few times and sent a few texts to friends, and the office had more than kept its promise by not contacting me once. Here it comes.

The phone flashed and buzzed over breakfast. The message read: 'hey Blondie here give us a call asap.' The dialling code was +507 – Panama, that cannot be good. It was enough to put me off my breakfast. Mind you, after last night's feast that was not difficult. What to do? I sent a message back asking for a good time to call; it seemed now was. Bugger. Mrs C. was just nursing a coffee and asked if there was a problem. I smiled and replied in the negative and explained my brother had reminded me again to bring him cigs. She laughed and said at least by smoking more he may become less of a fat bastard. Do not misunderstand this; it is the English way of expressing affection for someone.

Lady Luck had not yet deserted me; Anne had pushed away her coffee and said she was going back to bed. On the way back to the room she ran her finger along my back and suggested I come and wake her in 90 minutes or so to help work off last night's dinner.

Fair to say this was not the worst idea in the world. Okeydokey, can do. Here goes nothing.

Blondie answered straight away with a breathy, "Hello, my friend." He did not seem overly distressed.

I asked if everything was alright.

"Of course, my friend. I am reaping the fruits of our labour here in Panama."

At the least there were no problems with my part, and he sounded the same easy-going guy. We had a quick catch-up and then he asked where I was.

The answer seemed to make him even happier. A meeting was casually dropped into the conversation by him. Why not? It may be fun. My only condition was that Geert brought a date so it looked more natural. His condition was meeting in Tijuana in two days. It was not on our route but close enough to avoid suspicion, so I agreed. It could also add a little tang to the trip. Might just have sex first before I mention it to the missus.

The plan had been to move inland after San Diego; we were going to pop into Palm Springs then look for U2's tree in the Joshua Tree National Park. Hopefully we would find what we were looking for. After that, who knows? I fancied dipping into the Mojave Desert. Maybe we could throw this book into it and ask the dust. Then viva, to Vegas. Not bad, huh? Anne agreed that Mexico might be fun. Remember, this was the pre-millennium era; Mexico seemed safer back then. Yes, you had to be careful and smart, but where don't you?

Anyway, after another delirious day soaking up the sun in San Diego we travelled south of the border the following day. Bless Blondie, as he had booked us into the best room in the best hotel fully complementary. If memory serves, it was the Grande. The champagne was on ice and flowers addressed to Mrs C. festooned the room. With your limited knowledge, whatever you may think of him you cannot deny the man has style. The message light was flashing on the room phone, apparently there was a package for Señor Simon at the desk. Told you he had style – $9,999 in cash was waiting.

You are allowed to take ten thousand dollars in cash into the USA. My trip had just been paid for twice. Many foreigners travel to Tijuana to drink and dance, purchase bootleg brand-name and occasional tourist misbehaviour on the Revolución strip. However, Avenida Revolución has been known for its proliferation of nightclub shows, primarily catering to casual tourists. While still an entertaining town with an enjoyable atmosphere, locals and tourists alike would agree that it has lost its 'anything goes' mentality which it had once acquired – a shame. It is a mixed bag – good, bad, interesting with a hint of menace, but what is life without risk?

Blondie met us in the hotel bar with a dark, attractive, brooding companion in tow. No word of a lie, her name was Carmen Camilla Lopez. Not sure why we got the full name, I am guessing she insists on it. Another thing I was not sure about, was what Anne and I had done to her in a previous life. This was one unhappy bunny; all we got was brusque hola.

Geert made up for it with an exuberant welcome, then linking us both and leading us into the night. Carmen slunk after us, speaking machine-gun Spanish into her phone. How rude! If we say this was the first shock of the evening it may give the game away for the rest. Sure you will cope. The second shock was when I asked Blondie who Ms Lopez was and how he knew her. Guess what? Yes, it was a shock to find out it was his Columbian wife. Best not to ask. He just shrugged and smiled the fabled smile. The third was what a stroppy cow his wife was. The first restaurant suggested was met with a huff. When we went into a second it was not deemed good enough, with the host receiving an underserved volley of abuse from Mrs T. Finally, the third would apparently do. Looks like it could be a long, long night. Pause for a drink; more shocks after the starter.

My Spanish is passable, with Anne's at survival level, which was a good job as our attempts at conversation in English were met with a 'no hablo Ingles'. Her phone rang again and no one including her husband was upset when she went outside to answer it. Geert apologised, explaining that because she was not feeling well. Pooh, also she used indifference as a self-preservation tool because of her lack of English. Pull the other one. Also, she was shy. Yeah, right. We thanked him and told him not to worry. Which was true; her stroppiness was entertaining us and Geert's charm would suffice to ensure the evening went well.

As you know, myself and Mr Tromp are not big drinkers, however, remember his ability to snuff out problems? He did it again by ordering margarita pitches, which helped our Spanish and me avoid Carmen's blazing stare. Her eyes were burrowing into me for some reason. Fuck knows why. Even as she walks through the door, she can feel the eyes of the dark figure in the corner. Though she had a look of Salma Hayek, which is a good one, there was a danger and fire to her that while mesmerising, I was sure if you tried to get near you would get burned. She, like love, is a rebellious bird that nobody can tame, and it's all in vain to call it if it chooses to refuse.

The actual food was fab and our fun-loving Dutch

man had us in stitches. Thankfully his wife managed the odd sneer and frown but though present, managed to keep out of the way. It couldn't last, of course, what with the margaritas flowing and then a bottle of tequila landed on our table. Everyone has the drink that they dare not touch. For most it is the first thing that passed their lips as a wayward teen. So, cider, cheap wine, 20/20, or lousy lager. For me it was tequila. Though it was not my first drink, I had had three bouts with it and lost by a knockout each time. Anne shared my fear as she once called me in tears thanks to a tango with tequila. It got her lost in London way past the witching hour. The mystery of who ordered it was solved when Carmen opened it and drank from the neck of the bottle. This was yet another surprise, especially to Geert, whose eyebrows practically hit the roof.

The waiter was summoned by Ms Lopez and four glasses arrived and were quickly filled. Do you know what *venga y beba* means? Nor me. Mr T. blushed and sipped at his drink and was called a pussy for his efforts. Me and Anne got a, "Bebida, Gringos." That word I knew meant drink. Sorry to report that we rather let the British side down, both being called pussies. At least Carmen knew some English. She, of course, downed hers in one and even finished off her husbands for good measure. Her capriciousness may have impressed some, though there was a suspicion of vulgarity. She then spat some more Spanish at us. Blondie turned red; not surprising if my translation was correct. "Que te folle un pez," to my knowledge means she hoped we got fucked by a fish. Then we were told, "Eres tan patético que resultas entanable." Now we were all so pathetic, we were actually entertaining – charming.

Some women believe when they bear witness to unwarranted attacks, nasty comments or ignorant comments, look out! You're going to hear about it. It's not about causing unnecessary commotions, but shaking up the proverbial snow globe to keep people thinking and situations progressing. These are the women who will challenge conventional wisdom on how to behave. Thankfully these sailed over Mrs C's head as the margaritas' effect had left her oblivious to the change of energy in the room. Her eyes had glazed over and she had gone to another place. Sadly, Blondie and I were still relatively sober and were taking turns being abused by CCL. It was not clear at first why until she gingerly got to her feet after downing another class of tequila and shouted at me, "You have turned my man into a big soft pussy." At least it was in English. Colour me confused.

Geert shrugged, apologised again, and asked to meet me for breakfast, and then tried to catch up to Camila as she weaved out of the bar, abusing anyone in her way. Anne was now drooling on my soldier so had mercifully missed the final act. I knew my Dutch chum loved everything life had to offer; it also seemed he liked his ladies spicy, mixed with drama and a wide range of moods. Shame the missus had missed the tang in Tijuana.

CHAPTER 13

(Apt) The price you pay

The following morning I woke with a sense of foreboding which was not helped by the muggy humid air; it felt like a storm was on the way. Mr T. was pacing around in reception thankfully without his Colombian cruise missile in tow. He hugged me and we went to the terrace for a much-needed coffee. No smile – uh-oh. Geert got straight into his wife's behaviour the previous evening. "I love her, Simon." Synonym time. "She is robust, courageous, brilliant, intoxicating, formidable, dazzling, intense, and her courage and fatalism is so vividly realised that she would rather die than be false to herself." Praise indeed.

Back to the matter in hand as I had no problem with Blondie's choice of spouse. The issue on the table was what was her outburst all about. Though the location had changed, once again he informed me that crime was his true love and his real business. It appears his wife loved crime and danger more and hence him. He tried a smile and asked if I trusted him still.

This time it was not a strange question; in the current circumstances, I did. I broke my silence to ask as delicately as possible what sort of crime were we now talking about. Geert's tone became apologetic and he started to tell me about his other business, which given his wife's nationality should not be hard to figure out. Of course it was cocaine. This time I was extremely concerned about the above. "Fuck, Blondie, why?"

He explained that he did not get his hands dirty but did advise the Cali Cartel and had put them in contact with Dutch and Russian drug dealers. His job appeared to be more middle man than mad man. Still, this was way out of my league. I asked him if they knew about me. Well, that is why he wanted to meet me. At the moment my name had never been used and was not known by anyone apart from the G-men. They and Blondie liked me and wanted to keep me away from the dark side. "Simon, you are a great guy and I never wanted you dragged into this part of my life."

It begged the question then, why was I here now? He informed me that he wanted out, the big 'but' being **there was a price to pay to leave**. The first was Carmen, whose love of crime and danger far outweighed the love for her hubby. This explained her show-stopping outburst last night. The far bigger price, though, was that the Cali Cartel wanted help cleaning some cash.

"Simon, just help me one more time. I need you. One deal, a big RISK!" Bigger profit. Fuck!

The money was not going to cut it this time so I asked Geert what would happen if he did not help out. He explained no was not an option; he could run but these people could see for miles. So his friends and family would pay. No more G-men, no mum, no Carmen, so an upside and one more surprise, no more son. Oh yes, he had a son with the aforementioned Ms Lopez. Then after these people Mr Tromp would go down for the dirt nap. Finally his tone dropped to a whisper and he begged me to help get him out. **"Please, Simon. Like you, all I ever wanted was an easy life. Help me."** As always, our Dutch master was making a compelling case. After all, he was my friend and had been good to me and changed my life. Therefore there was a bond between us. Shit!

Mr T. interrupted my thoughts and told me to take my time and the smile became slightly more prominent as he said, "Fools rush in where angels fear to tread." Hard not to smile back.

We both sat back and had a drink of coffee in a comfortable silence. The silence did not remain golden for long as on the horizon marching at speed to us was Carmen Camila Lopez, with a stunt double who Blondie quickly informed me was her sister. He then said, "We may have a problem – she speaks English."

"What? Why?"

Blondie informed me Carmen knew our room details; they may have told Anne everything.

The rain began to fall, not exactly a clap of thunder but definitely a bad sign. The Colombian Bad Sister band were now nose-to-nose with Geert. Heaven knows what they were saying. The only word in the thousand volleyed in his direction I caught was cojones. Oh, balls. After a non-stop tirade the vocal guns were turned in my direction when the sister without mercy announced, "See how you like having your life fucked up, you English faggot." Carmen then spat at us both and off they popped. Nice to see you too, ladies. Please join us for lunch. All the colour had drained from the sky as well as both of our faces when in the gathering gloom I spotted Anne now readying an attack on our table. **What a morning.**

The coolest man in the Netherlands, maybe even Europe, had his head in his hands. I struggled out of my chair, patted him on the shoulder and told him to go and find his wife. I told him I'd call him around lunch when we had both had time to sort out melodramas.

He accepted gratefully and off he popped. In truth it would be better to deal with my wife without his presence. Now to describe what followed is not going to be easy. The problem is, I do not feel I have the literary talents to do the angst justice. Shakespeare could, he was good at drama and tragedy. Before we get to my feeble effort I could name drop a few esteemed authors into the mix. T.E. Lawrence – not only a great writer, also useful in a fight. John Fante – he dealt with a Camelia Lopez much better than me. There are of course many more. This may not be an obvious choice but as we have already given him a shout out for *Fever Pitch*, how about Nick Hornby? His tales of failed romance in *High Fidelity* is a personal favourite, more so as it was a gift from Anne. Sorry, just trying to put off recalling the darkness from that day. Whenever you have to write anything you could do worse than follow the advice from the late great Mrs Sumner (my old English teacher). Old school in every sense of the word. May your god bless you, Mrs S., wherever you are.

Write about what you know, write from the heart when you can, and remember, less is more.

Here goes. Based on the 'less is more' approach, Anne sat down, stood up and slapped me, sat back down, shouted, "Is it true?" and then those baby blues filled with water. What a worm.

Was it only a few days, or in your case, a few pages ago when we were sat in San Diego? Remember the warm, balmy evening air. The satisfaction of a full stomach, the sound of the ocean lapping in the background, then the person you love squeezes your hand and you get lost in their eyes. If you would like a further example of my despicability I even asked, "Is what true?"

Sorry about just using worm. How about 4, 8, and 9? Greed, Fraud and Treachery.

At that time it hit me what a complete and utter fool I was. No amount of money would compensate for the look on my wife's face. Why then, did I ask, "Is what true?" Oh, course it was true. Stupid. You know, she knew and I knew. That lost look, that hurt look, those eyes. I could feel the pain, the betrayal, the emptiness and the hurt. Yes, sorry. That was it. Yes, sorry.

So in my own words, is what true? Yes, sorry. You had better get hold of those Nobel and Booker people. Back to words. Anne had a few, if I may. "I cannot believe what you have done. First, you are not that clever, and who do you think you are? Was I not enough? You had me and it was not enough. You selfish, arrogant bastard. YOU HAD ME. Get me out of here, then we are done." After this, another slap and floods of tears.

In retrospect, it was not a good time for Blondie to reappear. The side of his face was bleeding, no doubt a gift from his loving spouse. His intentions may have been good but it was really not the time. Carman Camelia Lopez may have physically attacked him, now though, a verbal attack was about to head his way. Man the barricades. First, an apology to anyone from the Netherlands on behalf of myself and Anne. Let's say we forget political correctness when we are angry. He just managed that it was his fault, when Anne's eyes changed from blue to red and gave him the following instructions.

"You had better fuck off now, you clog-wearing, pancake-eating fraud. Go and stick your finger in a dyke and fuck some cheese, Geert. You have ruined my life."

I just shook my head and he did the wise thing and left us to it and headed to the bar. It was my turn to have my head in my hands; there were simply no words. There was a moment of just me and the sound of my own breath. The world seemed to stop for a second. I closed my eyes and wished to be anywhere else. It was not to be. Time to man up. Our eyes locked and there seemed to be some love left. Small comfort. Sorry, it is not possible to go into any more detail. We will have to go back to the 'less is more' approach and deal in some facts. Most of our things were locked in the car and we had only taken out the bare minimum for this trip, so packing in silence did not last as long as it seemed in the room. There was no point lying, so I told Anne I had to see Geert before we left. There was no answer and she headed to the bathroom. I heard the shower start so, sad to say, I headed for the bar. What a pair the two of us made in the bar. The dream team; bloody nightmare, more like. Blondie apologised again. There was no need, as eyes had been opened. We talked briefly and he agreed to come to London in a week to discuss his dilemma, we both needed a time out.

Guess your dreams always end. During the trip back to LA there was a toxic mix of silence and occasional cross examination of the last few months' activities. Here, the choice was to continue telling lies or go for the full confession. What could I say? What can I say? It would not change anything. To save us all driving along that highway, why bother even going there? The only thing that mattered that was true, is what Anne said earlier – I had had her and now I didn't. Enough.

Fortunately the airline was very accommodating (they usually are to their business-class clients). They offered us a flight back to London the following day so only one separate night in a soulless airport hotel to survive. Another sleepless night for me, for me, come back, come back, another sleepless night for me. As you can imagine the plane ride was not a happy one. I did not have the energy to ask for separate seats when I changed the dates so Anne and I were sat together but were an ocean apart. Like two strangers, our relationship was turning into dust. There was me and there was Anne. The only words were, "I thought I knew you," then a glance was exchanged, then nothing for the rest of the flight.

The phrase 'procrastination is the thief of time' has already been trotted out. I wish it was sat next to me as silence had pushed back time's tide. The silence seemed to follow me everywhere. My wife's love was fading. This was definitely a case of losing more than I had taken money-wise. A long-haul flight in every sense of the word.

CHAPTER 14

Ask the dust

To get away from the silence while we wait for our bags, some questions you may have.

Why did Geert bring Carmen?

An extremely good question and one of my first to him when the chance arrived. He had no choice. His assistant who booked the hotel let it slip, thinking it was a trip for the pair of them. It wasn't. He had planned to bring his assistant as a surprise. It sort of makes sense, best not dwell on it. Instead he did a beautiful famed Cruyff turn and told Carmen it was a surprise for her. He then had to book shows and various other activities to cover his tracks. You have already met Ms Lopez so it would come as no surprise to find out that she had pinned the assistant down, possibly literally, and got the hotel details from her. This was the first fuck-up. Yes, Carmen got ours and so was pissed from the start of the trip to find herself in another less salubrious hotel. Which it wasn't; still, she was rightly suspicious of a change in venue; her man should have not allowed them to be moved.

What a Gringo pussy; she wanted a macho man. Someone who took no shit and would die for her. Why book a different hotel? Such a rookie mistake. You met her; that woman could start a fight in an empty room. Also, Blondie still hoped to meet me without her in tow.

Wait a minute, didn't you ask him to bring a date?

Yes I did, but you know him, he is like a magnet to the ladies. He would have found someone. He is a real ladies' man. Testosterone on a stick.

Still some questions. How come CCL knew Blondie wanted out and why was it your fault?

Oh yes, another fair point. For argument's sake can we just say she did? He may have told her, or she may have got it out of him. Then the cunning Carmen must have put two and two together and come up with me when she first laid eyes on me in the hotel in Tijuana. It would explain her wild behaviour and that blazing stare that was combustible. Hope that clears everything up for the time being. Our bags are here; let us return to the silence.

At least when we walked into the arrivals hall there was one smile in the crowd which belonged to John, my affable brother-in-law. He hugged his sister and warmly greeted me. Hum, there may be still be a flicker of hope. I was not the only one confused by his presence as his first words were, "So why am I here, sis?" It had been what seemed an Ice Age since Anne last spoke so her voice sounded a little strange; there was none of the usual life. There were only sad, monotone, flat words informing her brother that I had to go back to work and as she didn't she could spend some time with her mother.

Quickly, before we continue, John lives near their parents and they are all a close family. Honestly, you people. Thankfully among her brother's many qualities, curiosity is not one of them, if curiosity can be described as such.

He just made a joke about having to get his money out of the bank if his idiot brother-in-law was needed in such haste. Not bad, though it was not good idea to smile. Can you feel the cold, hard stare chilling my every fibre and bones? Anne explained to John that as she had most of her things there was no need to go home, so it would be easy to go straight back to her parents'. All he did was shrug and say, "Fine," and offered to take her bags to the car to give us a chance to say a proper goodbye. John wrote the parking bay number on his sister's hand and then did a very disturbing tongue kissing mime before bursting into song, singing. "Simon and Anne, up a tree, K. I. S. S. I. N. G." God love him.

We had returned to stilted silence and despite my efforts, Anne wanted to leave without another word. This was no way to end so I pulled out the big gun. It was time for the late great Ian Curtis (again). Well, his words anyway. "Annie, don't walk away in silence, see the danger, always danger, don't walk away."

I got a hesitant, "Okay." I don't care what you say, you cannot whack Joy Division. We sat down on the first empty seats we could find. It was my turn for some questions. About time, if you ask me. Not being sure how long the truce would last, I fired out the following, "Can you ever forgive me? What about the future, the house? Do you need money?"

There was no reply. Okay, okay, too insensitive. "Mrs Anne Carroll, can you at least help me with one thing? Should I help Geert?" This completely threw my wife. At last, a look that did not chill me to the core of my being. It was a nice old puzzled look. There may even have been some concern in those beautiful blue eyes. Oh, how I miss those eyes. It appeared my question time was over. It was time for answers. After a few truths I explained my dilemma with Geert, Stomp, Mr Tromp, Cruyff, Blondie, Erasmus, and Frans. Believe it or not, if she had told me to walk away and not help out I would have and that would have been that. The End. Alas, Ms Lawrence as she now is, did not. So a man has to do what his wife tells him to do. Regarding my marriage, it got shot in Tijuana and was now dead on arrival back in Britain. If it is okay, can we leave the wreck of my marriage in the arrivals area at Heathrow? Please do not ask which terminal, check online if you care so much. Sorry. It is still raw.

The fall from grace, to have loved and to have lost, where things were never going to be the same. All forms of contact had been ignored; the game seemed well and truly up. Even her mother, who was my biggest fan outside mine, did not want to intervene. When I called she was her usual charming self but would not say where her daughter was, just she did not want to speak to me. Bless her though, she did ask after my and tell me to be look after myself. She also hoped we could work it out. Good old Christine, hope she is alright. To try and cleanse my soul I spent a few days with my parents. They did not give me the third degree on my wife's whereabouts, they were just pleased to have me around for a few days. It did help; between my dad calling me Andrew (my brother) and my mother following me round the house asking if I was hungry, it took me out of myself for a bit.

Feel like there should be an ominous sound here, as we have used the weather metaphor. Blondie was back in the country; may as well go and see if he is as miserable as me. Think he was, but here were of course several words of wisdom. "We only have one life, my friend. Do you want to spend the rest of it apologising, regretting, hating yourself? Do you fuck; even a happy life cannot be without a measure of darkness. The word happy would lose its meaning if it were not balanced by sadness. It is far better take things as they come along. Simon, difficult roads often lead to beautiful destinations, **let's embrace this last risk**."

Please make a note of this, especially that word 'last', as this may not be the last time we hear it. He did not ask if I was going to help him, he knew it. Why else would I meet him? Fair to say he had my number. Get your passports out again, we will be off soon!

You may want to consult your government's website first though, due to our next port of call.

The Foreign and Commonwealth Office (FCO) advise against all travel to Colombia. Despite improvements in security, crime rates remain high. Illegal armed groups and other criminal groups are heavily involved in the drugs trade and serious crime, including kidnapping (for ransom and political purposes), money laundering, and running extortion and prostitution rackets. The British Embassy has received reports of criminals in Colombia using drugs to subdue their victims. This includes the use of scopolamine, which temporarily incapacitates unsuspecting victims. Drugs can be administered through food, drinks, cigarettes, aerosols, and even paper flyers. Victims become disoriented quickly and are vulnerable to robbery, sexual assault, and other crimes. Avoid leaving food or drinks unattended and don't take anything from strangers. Where possible, plan how you will travel to and from your destination. Only use pre-booked taxis. Be wary if you are approached by a stranger. In many areas the authority of the Colombian State is limited, and the British Embassy's ability to help British nationals in trouble in these areas will also be limited.

What could possibly go wrong?

CHAPTER 15

What am I doing here?

Nothing, according to Geert. He had a different spin on the trip. Apparently Columbia is emerging from the civil unrest. Colombia has established itself as one of the world's must-see destinations. It is exquisite. Blessed with natural beauty. Think Andean mountains, Caribbean beaches, Amazon jungle, and thriving cities. My favourite bit now. It's a joy to travel around and is a place full of hip bars, street art, vibrant markets, and colourful architecture. You are going to love it. Your call; I will meet you in the airport if you are coming. I got there before my friend and passed the time reading *Killing Pablo* by Mark Bowden. When Blondie saw me he laughed out loud (or LOL for the kids) and called me a Fucking Gringo pussy. Before we set off, do I have to pay these authors mentioned, or do they pay me?

We have gone through security now, nearly beyond the point of no return. Time for a quick drink. Two tonic waters please. Mr Tromp and I like to drink tonic water for a few reasons.

First, it gives out the appearance of sophistication. Second, it is non-alcoholic but does not appear so to the onlooker. Finally, there is quinine in it, which may help ward off the onslaught of mosquitoes. Possibly the least of our worries. They have called our fight; head back, eyes closed, deep breath and exhale. Bye Anne.

I had sent her a letter as my final roll of the dice in an attempt to at least express some words. When we were dating I used to send her handwritten letters all the time, which she even admitted to quite enjoying. Her roommate at the time, Ruth, let the cat out of the bag though, by informing me she used to run downstairs to check and grinned from ear to ear when they arrived.

To: Anne Lawrence

Anne

I am now deservedly in pain and miss you in SW1. It is quite strange and hope never to get used to it. Geert and I fly midweek and I hope to be home as soon as possible. Thank You for being my wife and hope you are okay. How is work taking your decision to leave? It has been an odd year and confusion still reigns for me. If you remember my father's words at my uncles funeral, though they maybe Vera Lynn's Hope we will meet again, don't know where don't know when but I hope we will meet again some sunny day. Please take care and thanks for making me a better man for a while. I will never feel alone in the world thanks to the memory of you.

Simon

X

Two days later an email came which I still have today.

Simon

You have done lots of things that I don't understand and can't cope with, but the fact remains that I have always thought you were a kind person. Everyone has been positive which makes me feel happier about my decision. If you can get in touch with your mum and dad to let them know when you are coming back I would do as I am sure they are worried. I am going to Madrid this weekend, last holiday I will be having for a long while! Don't want to ask you too many question as I am afraid I am not going to like the answers, but I am glad you are helping your friend despite what I said to him he is a good guy. Take care and don't forget to come back! Sorry but it is goodbye,

Anne.

There we have it. Conclusive enough for you? It was for me, which made making the trip to Colombia more of a fait accompli.

Guess me and Blondie are the fools rushing in where angels fear to tread. Sat on the plane now, eyes down, breath slow, here goes nothing. It may sound a tad dramatic but the will to live, if not totally gone was reduced enough to head into the unknown. Unknown was the right word for our travel plans, as Mr Tromp has several rules of international travel.

Rule one: never fly direct to your final destination.

Rule two: never tell anyone where you are going.

Rule three: never use the same airline unless

absolutely necessary.

Rule four: do not talk to anyone you do not know.

There are more, which we will save for later. If you were going to Colombia where would you fly first? Mexico, USA, Venezuela, or maybe Peru. Oh no, we were going to Canada first. At least it began with C. Just a few hours in Toronto then on to Mexico. Olé. Now we are off to Ecuador. I wish I could tell you something about these places. Sadly, a mixture of fear and lack of time means my memory of these destinations is limited to airport terminals and one airport hotel. On the upside, the flying part of the journey was over. We were going to drive from Quito to Cali. There is of course a downside; it may look close on a map but it is a distance of over 700km or 430 miles in Church of England dominations. That is over fifteen hours without stopping. We'd better be bloody stopping. Blondie and I had not spoken much on the flights as we were both knackered and slept and read or watched films. This was not a problem as we were extremely comfortable in each other's company. He did not seem overly stressed and did manage to flirt with a few of the flight attendants, which was quite comforting in a strange way. The plan was to get the car and drive to the border, and get into Colombia as soon as possible. Blondie had arranged the car, which was bloody huge. It was some type of 4X4 SUV with blacked-out windows, de rigueur for this part of the world. I have seen smaller flats in London. My reaction on seeing this monstrosity on wheels made us both laugh so the journey started well. Up to this point I had not asked Geert what exactly my role was going to be, so now seemed as good a time as any. That bloody smile was back; he explained that he needed me to talk to me. Enigmatic to the core. Still, who does not like to talk to themselves? What he meant was that all I had to do was to talk to the Cali Cartel's financial chap. Apparently he had been educated in the USA; Princeton, according to Geert.

My job was to give him the SP on how to move some of the money and look at what he was doing, and if required point him in the right direction. It did not seem so bad so I relaxed immeasurably. The Dutch daredevil had to do the dirty work, so it seemed. Good. Positive he will be fine, I'm sure they are like little kittens compared to Carmen Camilla Lopez. Speaking of whom, Blondie informed me that if I was not such a white-collar pussy I would be quite cute according to his mad missus. What? What indeed. No word of lie, in the odd sparing minutes when she was not frothing at the mouth while trying to kill her hubby, she told him I was cute.

Well, well, well. It would be like stroking a rabid tiger or some other crazy wild animal. That would be more creative than the former description. It did keep the car ride a jolly one though. Me and Carmen, up a tree, K. I. S. S. I. N. G. Bet there is a tiger at the bottom of it, or knowing my luck, in it. We all know Stomp (not used this name for a while, though did explain) is fab company, so there we were. I told him he was Thelma and I was Louise. He weighed in with Butch and Sundance. Thought they were in Bolivia? Still, good one. Then I dropped in the fact that he was the doppelgänger of Rutger Hauer. Oh yeah? So who wouldn't shit themselves with the Hitcher on their trail? Threw in a spot of reminiscing, then a bit of teasing about our respective marriages, and before you knew it we were at the border.

First, an apology to the residents of Ecuador as I did not really take in much of the scenery on the drive. This was not intentional; afraid we were having a good time chatting. This goes out to Elizabeth Achig, a close Ecuadorian friend of mine. Good luck with the new website and if you need any help with the Swiss, let me know. Next up, an apology to any Colombian national who should stumble across this text. I do have to mention, though, that our time at your border was cut considerably by Frans (get what I'm doing?) doling out notes to the guards. This sped up our passage through immensely. We sailed through. We decided to stop in Ipiales which is close to Ecuador's border. The town itself was rather an uninspiring commercial town so I did wonder why Erasmus had brought me here.

Back to Geert and Blondie soon, just have to update you now and again. It would be foolish to question the man/men as he has fantastic taste, especially in friends. For a start the staff in the hotel fell over themselves to make our stay a happy one. Next, the food in the nearby restaurant was exquisite. The señoritas were none too shabby either. Who needs TV when you can look into their sultry faces and admire their non-surgical curves, hair like ink on white parchment, and the untamed spirit that shines through? For your information I just looked, best not ask about Blondie.

In the morning we took a detour to the nearby Las Lajas cathedral. Ah, good old Geert. This is why we are here. It's a stunning building that spans a massive gorge and it's well worth stopping at should you be in the vicinity. In my opinion the best views are from the path on the other side of the gorge. Excuse me, Mr/Ms Editor, could we stick a picture in here? It will save me a few words. Whether it was from the previous evening's activity or for some guidance in general, Blondie went in and lit a candle and bowed his head. Okay then, when in Rome. I bowed my head as well. My friend was muttering to himself; it had been a while for me. What can you say in these situations? Sorry, forgive me, I settled for the Lord's Prayer and asked for help. Sorry God. If you are listening please make me a better man and make sure Anne is alright. Sorry about the path I am on. It appears that I am not afraid of dying but I am afraid of going to hell. Do not worry, we are not far away from it.

The cathedral was a comfort; you could hear the buzz of the silence all around. Very therapeutic. When we got outside the smile was out with an explanation of being a lapsed Catholic forthcoming from the lips of that fated smile. LAPSED, blimey, not even a thesaurus can help us here. It offers up one time, erstwhile and lost. Wait, we have failed. Look who's talking. Let's move on.

We lunched in a town called San Juan de Pasto, or Pasto for short, known by the locals as the Surprise City. The biggest surprise was that we had roasted guinea pig for lunch washed down with a diabetes-inducing passionfruit drink – pure sugar. Sorry, but yuk! For an Englishman my palate is quite adventurous and I have tried many dishes on my travels. Roasted guinea pig now replace grasshoppers at the bottom of the list. Even Geert was gagging. Ha, just when the waitress was flashing him a smile; perfect timing, live one.

We are on the road again, heading to the White City. Not the dog track but a place called Popayan. That was to be our base for the evening and then we'd plan the big push into Cali. The drive was not a smooth one; the road was packed and we both had to decorate the side of the road with the remnants of lunch several times. Still, I won – only twice to Geert's three. There were no bluebirds over the outskirts of White City; however, there were vultures in the sky. Just trying to build up the tension. Not convinced? How about the two black cars that have appeared in my mirror. Now one has overtaken us and is in front and the brake lights are on. Oh dear.

Time for a commercial break. Get yourself a cup of tea and biscuit and take a breather. Go on. You deserve it if you have got this far. In fact you, may never have to read any of the previous twaddle. This is the point where we print this off and send it out. I did send the text at 5,000 words to several publishers. Only one answer so far:

Many thanks for sending in Don Simon. I'm afraid though that I didn't feel we could publish it successfully at Cape. Good luck with the book.

Could be worse; personally I feel it grows on you, so fingers crossed. This could be the end of the road, in the story or in this venture. How right can you be? Nobody loves it, everybody hates it, think I will go and eat worms. For a full run down see the front or back or both.

Shall we return to the road in Colombia? I hope you are still with us. No. Many others feel the need; ah, this may be a chance to get angry or even. I do not have the inclination to do anything but blindly carry on. The text and style are all over the place; still, some may find some genius in the madness or it may even fall into the 'so bad it is good' category. Death or glory or at least let us try and make it to the end together.

So, I am driving. In front of us is a large black car with tinted windows and the brake lights are on. The car behind is trying to make love to our bumper. Blondie does not seem overly concerned. Both cars get closer, the only option is to stop. This is the point where Thelma and Louise drive into the gorge. It is also the point where Butch and Sundance charge at the might of the Bolivian army. We had a car to the left of us and a car to the right of us. What to do, what to do? We got out together, then the door of the car in front swung open. Is this it? The door to the next life, too dramatic? This is such nonsense. Calm, for a start, as is Mr T.

A blond-haired head is now visible out of the car. Not your average Colombian assassin. Hard to see in the light but the profile emerging looks about four feet tall. We may be alright here. I turn to Blondie and his smile is as big as I have ever seen it. The tiny figure is running towards us; the figure is not getting any bigger but the smile is. Now I see why. He is a Geert clone – his son. The boy jumps into my friend's arms and find myself moved and reassured by all of this. Several minutes of hugging, kissing, and the like followed. Oh, those continentals and their feelings.

The most affection shown to me was the odd pat on the head from my parents, just as it should be. Finally, after he had put his son down I was introduced to Master Johan Tromp. He greeted me in Spanish, then Dutch, and the little sod settled on English. Not a big fan of kids, still, he seemed to make my friend happy.

Now was not the time to ask about all the drama; sure it would become clear later. I drove into town while father and son chatted away in the back. We also had a two-car convoy as insurance. For those who have stuck with me from the start, this is and will not be the last time you will see 'What the hell am I doing here?'

CHAPTER 16

The Big Mig

Not sure if it is stereotypical to take a siesta in Spanish-speaking countries, but I needed one.

Blondie assured me the hotel was the best in town when we checked in. That may have been the case but what was the deal with the air-con? The choice – peace and quiet and heat or noise and comfort. Picked the latter and had a fitful sleep. Over dinner the reality of our situation became clearer – the cars. Anyone with money is a target so Johan was driven everywhere with security and as Europeans we would now need it too. Remember the title of the last chapter. Cali, here we come.

After breakfast where further conversation was not possible due the precocious Master Tromp, we walked out of the hotel where there were now five cars waiting for us. What the bloody hell is going on now? Never fear, the anxiety buster was behind me with a soothing explanation. The less contact I had with the chaps in Cali the better, no argument there.

My job was to meet the American, as Blondie called him, and talk finance. The stress buster strikes again. Therefore, as well as being driven there I would also have a one-car escort. I managed a smile and asked why Blondie got a two-car escort and there was just the one for me. That laugh, that smile, then a pat on the back – it had been a while since the last pat. So, calm again for now.

You could have chilled wine in the car – it was bliss after my air-con problems the day before. Told the driver he should hire it out to soft Europeans. Not a flicker; my Spanish is not that bad so it looked like a silent journey into Cali. Tried one more interaction by asking about the journey time and got the finger. Well, three of them. Sod it, may as well have a sleep. Before I went into Sleepsville I asked the driver to wake me twenty minutes from town so I could get suited and booted. I did get a "Si, señor." Wow, he may not kill me. So I fell into a deep sleep. A good sleep, still alive, but still in the car in Cali in Colombia. Cock.

Dressed to impress, I arrived at the Marriot in Cali. Should get a decent lunch at least, no roasted guinea pig.

Another well-dressed man was waiting for me (come on, my suits come from Savile Row) at reception. He introduced himself as Todd; he seemed okay. He is – sadly, was (more later). We sized each other up over a rather pleasant lunch with business not brought up. Like me, Todd was in way over his head and like me, he mentioned (here we go again), "What the hell am I doing here?" Sorry, it will be a continuing theme for a while. His background was a

US version of mine; reasonably well educated, smooth, handsome (you get that one). He, like me, had managed to climb the greasy pole to the heights where the rewards were good but left you wanting more. You can guess the rest; he met a guy who knew a guy who knew a group who offered no-risk riches. Now we were in the same shit together.

Whatever tension there may have been had gone and we were enjoying each other's company and laughing at our plight. After lunch we got down to business. Todd knew his stuff Stateside and I clued him in on Singapore, and we seemed to be coming from the same place.

He stole the Godfather 3 line, 'just when you think you are out they drag you back in.'

We know he is not the only one guilty of stealing words. Speaking of which, Blondie had just arrived in a motorcade that any president would be proud of. Todd asked me who the hell he was. "Believe it or not, Todd, this is good news. At least we are going to have a fun night out."

Blondie looked tired and drawn and just about raised a smile. The spirit was still there though. He offered his hand to our new American amigo, mentioned a siesta then a fiesta. We tied up some loose ends and best of all, Todd agreed to do the presentation. I still feel bad about this as it may have appeared yellow on my part. The night out was a merry one; you cannot help thinking if you could take away the crime or the fear of crime, what a great place Cali could be. We dined, drank (a little), and even danced. Of course Geert moved like a gazelle while Todd and I shuffled about occasionally waving an arm here and an arm there. Then there was the women, wow! The way they move, the hair, the eyes – pure class. Close again, but still in mourning so just about passed. It was just fun to bump and grind a little and even had my arse pinched a few times. All in all, a top night and much needed by all concerned.

The three amigos, as we had christened ourselves last night, were minus two of their members at breakfast; there was just me, only the lonely. Before we move on, a special mention to the staff at the Marriot in Cali. Top notch, made all of us feel very welcome. I was looking forward to the tales and especially from the blond one, as if Carmen is in town I want to tell her the good news and then run like hell. As there was just me, the waitress was flashing a lovely smile and bringing me fresh coffee. Not quite sex for breakfast but close enough for now. Maybe I should have stayed in the church a few days ago.

Go back a bit for name and location. The pleasant ambiance around me was about to end as six serious-looking men had entered and were prowling around. Thank God they walked straight past my table. They then treated the ensemble breakfast diners to a very convincing Marx brothers routine. They poked each other and began bickering like old women at the bingo. Better than the telly. It was great entertainment for a bit, though this was not a good time for the other two amigos to come in. They called Todd Gringo One and told him to get lost, and told Geert, or Gringo Two, to join them in reception. Oh, one more – what am I doing here?

Todd seemed calm enough, must be last night's sex. He explained the blokes were on our side. Oh, marvellous. After a blow-by-blow account of his exploits we went to a conference room to finalise what we hoped was a presentation pitch that would mean a peaceful way out. The third amigo joined us two hours in and seemed impressed with our work. My offer to accompany them was thankfully turned down. Bless you both. The pretty breakfast waitress was still on duty so though I lunched alone, it did not feel that way. What a smile. It melted my cold, lonely, broken heart. Bless her, she smiled and smiled and brushed my hand, sending a charge to my presently unemployed crotch. Bad time for Mr Charm AKA Blondie to breeze back in. My latest flame looked but her smile refocused on me, 1-0 to England. He did not notice. There was news, good and bad. The good was the financial advice had gone down a storm, the bad news, there was a party at some place or other held by the so-called Cali KGB. Can't wait, Blondie. He tried to reassure me, saying they had a few British mercenaries on the books so it would be easier to blend into the background.

Great. I am going to ask a question myself here. If I can blend into the background why do I have to go? It appeared Todd was a bit nervous today with the Q&A and Blondie wanted me around to answer any questions he couldn't. Nice to be needed and wanted. On that score, a wise man once told me that your god gives you what you need, not what you want. Quite sure I neither want or need to go to this party. This was not the plan, never mind the dream.

Looking at Todd's face as he joined us, it was not where he had planned to be. He was one of those annoyingly handsome off-the-peg Americans. Tall, dark, well-built – Clark Kent without the glasses. He was not acting like Superman at present, he was moaning and begging Blondie to get him out of the night's shindig. His bleating was rewarded with a compromise of a one-hour show-your-face tour; toast the host, then do one. After he left, looking relieved, I felt the need to defend him to Geert who looked like he was about to utter something disparaging. Instead he nodded and made me smile despite myself saying The Todd needed a time out. The Todd – good one, Dutchman. Sure as day follows night and vice versa, the evening arrived. Another question. Can't these Colombians go anywhere in just one car?

The party was at some estate or other, best not ask where or who it belonged to. All you need to know was the driveway to the house was long and there appeared to be armed men lining it, just what the doctor ordered if he ordered you to be shot. The place was thronged with people; some acknowledged Geert, none me. Yeah, and one or two to The Todd, much to his discomfort. An hour may be too much for him at this rate. We were escorted through the main party area into what must have been the VIP area. Lucky us! Two people now acknowledged me. "Hola Gringo." I smiled and replied that I preferred my full name of Señor Gringo Pussy. Believe I may just have made Carmen and her equally delightful sister smile. 2-0 England. I lost concentration and hung around, which gave Carmen time to ask about Anne. England 2, Colombia 1. I smiled and moved on. Better park the bus somewhere else and hang on.

Mr Tromp was behind me and ushered his darling wife to another area, leaving me with his sister-in-law.

She was seductive in a 'stick your hand in the fire' type way. She tossed her magnificent mane and leaned into me and brought her lips to my ear. Hello, hello. Then before my loins could react, her voice poured cold water into my ear by whispering, "I bet you are shitting yourself, Englishman."

Now what would David Niven say? What would John Le Mesurier say? For they themselves have said it, and it is greatly to their credit that they are Englishmen. For in spite of all temptations to belong to other nations, they remained Englishmen. Wish Blondie was around so I could borrow his smile. I tried my best and replied, "On the contrary, Carmen Camelia Lopez's sister, I feel quite at home."

She spat out her name, "Maria Lopez," then asked me why.

So, with a big grin I said, "My dear Ms Maria Lopez, we are surrounded by ex-British special forces, some of whom were in my father and brother's regiment. It is you, my dear, who should be shitting it, as you so crudely put it, though sure it would spoil your divine dress." 3-1. Oh, the look she gave me was priceless. It may have even equalled the cost of the party. She declined my offer of a drink and stomped off. She had gone to the other side of the room to be closer to Carmen. I waved at them, ha. Blondie came over to my side and asked what the hell had happened. I just smiled. Ah, another pat on the back.

The party had been quire sophisticated so far, however, there now seemed to be a lot of bickering going on with some of the shall we say 'gold chain wearing' macho guests. It was not quite on a par with my breakfast show; still, not bad. The Todd was now by mine and Blondie's side, and had got a tick from somewhere. Geert as always knew before he did and sent him back to the hotel. You could almost see the weight lift off his shoulder as he hurried from the room. He was almost drawn into the tiff in the room on the way out but managed to mutter an apology before sprinting for his freedom. The rest of the room had now fallen silent, as the tiff seemed to be developing into a full-on fracas. Blondie sighed and said, "They are arguing about money, they are always fighting about money."

A few slaps and pushes now interrupted the shouting. Blimey, this could get nasty; that is until three rather distinguished-looking gentlemen came in and the room returned to a respectful hush, thank heavens for that. These men were the real deal, as I may have seen someone curtsey. They were heading our way. They must have been important as Carmen and Maria were now by our side. Believe it or not, Carmen was looking at hubby with something other than her usual scorn and mad Maria linked my arm, cheeky mare.

The gentlemen were now upon us. They greeted Blondie as the Dutchman, acknowledged the satanic sisters, and the best groomed of the lot introduced himself to me. He told me his name was Miguel and his group were to be called the Cali Gentlemen. In hindsight it would have been wise to simply smile, say yes sir no sir, but the client advisor side of me was kicking in. Miguel certainly looked and acted like one of my bank's clients. He had a look of good old Jean Pierre. You know, my French Casanova client. So I said, "Good evening, Cali Gentlemen, and good evening Miguel," trying my best David Niven, then said, "Jolly nice to meet you fellows," doing my best JLM.

Miguel smiled and said, "You have to be the Englishman. Nice plan. Please join us for a drink."

Maria was now squeezing my arm and brushed an imaginary hair off my shoulder. Hum, two can play at that game, so I gave her firm arse a squeeze with my free hand. Thong. Nice. Damn, she kept her cool, though I'm sure the invoice is in the post and the repayment terms will not be favourable. The rest of the party parted to let us through and we sat down. The other gentlemen did not give out their names and though they chatted amiably with me and the Dutchman, Miguel raised his glass and toasted the English. Oh, Maria's face again, this time a slapped not squeezed arse. It seemed he was a big fan so I mentioned mine and Blondie's love of afternoon tea and even blagged him about footy for a while. He was handsome and did care, so could be a charming man too. The gentlemen were cagey but good company, so much so that I felt brave enough to ask about the car situation, much to the group's amusement. They hit back, verbally thankfully, telling me horse-drawn coaches would not cut it in Cali. We chatted a little and for a while more until the mystery man rose followed by Miguel. Just before he left, Miguel said, "I like U2, Dutchman." Englishman was tempted to do a Bono joke but I had pushed my luck enough for one night so thanked him and Blondie praised the party.

Handshakes all round, kisses for the sisters, then they were gone. I smiled at Maria and said, "My place or yours." Multiple choice. A – Kiss. B – Slap. C –

Smile. Call if you care.

Carmen and Geert are now kissing, sadly not up a tree but in front of Maria and me. We were both in agreement, screaming, "Yuk! Get a room." This seemed to go on for a terminally long time, then there was a spell of whispering and amazingly I got another smile from Ms Lopez and she led her sister away so Geert and I could talk.

"Simon, my friend, I knew you were our guy. Well done." You may have seen this line before, never ever tire of it personally.

It was my turn to talk and I asked him if his plan was still the same given his recent bout of tonsil tennis with his wife. Can you hear my sigh of relief? You should, as despite his irrational love of CCL he wanted out more; he hoped she would join him somewhere else but getting out clean and alive was still his main priority.

We talked some more and drew up our escape plan. It was for me and Blondie to go to Panama. I'd set up some accounts and do the IT, Geert would stay for Cali's man and any cash transfer. Todd would line up a few cash-poor US companies then tie up a US-Dutch transfer. Singapore was my next port of call with more electronic wizardry. Geert to the Cayman Isles, then we were all to meet up in Amsterdam with the G and this time, please, that should be that. Talk about fools rushing around and in. What could possibly go wrong?

We hugged and I made my way out, waving to my new gal pals and saluting the Cali Gentlemen, and was chuffed that Miguel and his men reciprocated. A four-car escort – not sure whether to be pleased or chilled to my very core.

On arrival at the hotel I found Todd slumped in a chair in the bar. "Come on, Todd, it went well. We are nearly there now." At that time I believed this and still thought I could win Anne back, so I told him about our trip along highway one and tried to put him in his dream car going to his dream location. It did the trick; he perked up no end and we spent another night on the town. USA 2, Columbia 0. Coach Carroll still on the bench.

Only the lonely again at breakfast; even my waitress was nowhere to be seen. All of the other hotel guests must have been at the party as the restaurant was deserted.

Depression was kicking in and I was about to drown in a wave of self-pity. Some may have envied my current lifestyle but being in an empty room bereft of people, loneliness had me in its grip. After Anne had left me, I had stopped thinking about the future, so when this deal was done, who knew what lay ahead. There would be no need to work and so free in some ways, but just free to be by myself. Oh shut up, Simon.

Todd turned up. Sex sure did agree with him; he was twice the man he used to be yesterday. He was again going into far too much detail. Still, we needed The Todd to be on top form back in the USA. The fact he was going home today had taken his cares away; he could taste his freedom so gave breakfast a miss. We talked over the plan and it was the happiest I had seen him on the whole trip.

We all met up at Cali airport, including my new best friends, the Lopez liggers. The Todd had read the Tromp guide to travel and was going to stop in Mexico one night before heading home. I flashed a grin at the Lopezes and told him to avoid Tijuana. We both gave him a manly pat on the back and he was on his way. It was our turn next, but not before the Tromps were at it again. Oh, come on. I offered my lips to Maria.

We of course were not going direct to Panama. Cali to Caracas to Costa Rica, then another silly SUV My stay in Panama was mercifully short, in fact I think it was roughly the same as the time it took to get there. My only duty was to line up a couple of friendly banks and the last one, the First Inter Americas bank, gave me free reign. This became clearer when the manager who had already given up his desk and office for me, said, "Señor Miguel sends his and the Gentlemen's regards." Bloody hell, dancing with the devil here. I thanked him and asked him to pass on the Dutch and Englishman's best wishes, and said to say 'pip, pip'.

Caught up with Geert in the hotel and wished him the best and headed out of there. Had a day or more in the air to overcome. Money-wise, I had not asked for any on this deal and was sure Blondie had done the same. He had given me some walking around cash and had booked me first class all the way, but that was it. Not sure about Todd; he reported to the Cali Gents so we left him to it. If they are not paying you, they may forget you.

I did promise travel at the start; well, you are about to get more than you can take. A six-hour stopover in

Mexico City, up to Atlanta, did overnight and met The Todd. USA 3; he, like Blondie likes the ladies. Glad to see him, happy and care-free Todd on the tear. Next stop, LAX. Just a two-hour stop then the big long flight to Tokyo. Thank heavens for first class. Never been so spent, the day and an uneventful evening hardly lost in translation. Does anyone know what day it is? What time is it? So jet lagged that I spent the night walking Tokyo's neon-lit streets which was quite similar to walking around a sci-fi film set. Finally got back to my hotel room and still could not sleep so spent the night blinking at the brightly lit city of Tokyo. Las Vegas has nothing on it. I had considered staying another day but there was just too much to see and do and I was not in the right frame of mind to attempt the task. Another time, Tokyo.

Singapore next. We have been here before and it was such a great trip. Gareth, Amanda, and Anne, guess you should not go back. Blondie had booked me into Raffles which should serve as an oasis to provide me with calm during my short stay. I's dotted, T's crossed, deal done. Next Dubai, then the Dam.

Dubai was seen as a playground of the rich, however, it has opened the doors to the masses recently. Although much of the place is ultra-modern in construction and design, it does not do it for me. Geert had arranged the trip and had suggested all manner of luxury hotels in town. The Burj Al Arab hotel was still under construction. You know, the famous pointy one in the sea. So I passed and settled on the Dunes Hotel Apartments close to the airport and just tried to get close to GMT. Eat, sleep, and repeat then ready to re-join the G-men.

CHAPTER 17

Oh, Todd!

More than happy to be back in Old Amsterdam, guess this is where it all started. Would it be too obvious to say I hope this is where it all ends? It felt like I had been in the air forever so I was extremely cheered to find Vinny and Jan waiting for me at Schiphol. It was good to see them and I was even more cheered when we took the train into town. They smiled and told me the main man had regaled them with my tales of Colombia and cars. Great lads, good to be back.

In town they took me to an Amsterdam coffee shop – not that sort, proper coffee and cakes and a few laughs. They had already muffled apologies on the train about their failure to mention the Cali connection. I had accepted this in good grace and we had all moved on, or back, if the fun we were having was anything to go by. They had just laid down some tickets to an art exhibition that evening that had tickled us all. HB joined us and we all said, "Fuck it, let's go." It could be fun, an arty-farty show to forget.

It was. Lots of style and good taste.

Before we move to breakfast, a question. Sorry. I love Anne and possibly always will, but it has been a while. The act of betrayal was heinous and I hate the hurt that I caused. Still, have not had a bit for a month or so. Would it be alright with you if my flesh weakens? Please do not answer as I already know. Just last night was not only a classy affair, there were lots of lovely ladies in their LBDs. Yum; my favourite. One even referred to me as an elegant Englishman. The G-men thought I was mad when I went back to the hotel alone.

Dare I drag it out again? Sod it. As it was early I spent the morning just people watching, something that never seems to lose its appeal, especially in foreign climes. There is also a pleasant feeling of anonymity when you are in another country. Time though, like the proverb says, does not wait for any man, so I had to run to meet our fun-loving G-men. At least the people change.

We had passed on the business yesterday, but some had to be done today. Everything had gone to plan and the final piece was easy. Believe it or not they had another warehouse stuffed with cash that was to be handed over to the Cali Gents in return for an electronic transfer to Zurich, sadly set up by me. Like the G, the C loved their lolly loose – it seemed they needed some walking around cash for some European operation or other.

My friend Fran was back in town. Hugs and pats all round, then he gave me a case. Oh no, not another case of cash. My cut from them to me. I remained calm but calmed more when Vinny informed me that it was nothing to do with the CCG. The least I could do was invite them out for dinner. Raw fish anyone?

Blondie was late for dinner, the master of timing. Still, me and the boys were laughing it up. Then he arrived, ashen faced and not a smile in sight. Shit. He beckoned me out of the restaurant with an urgent wave. Vinny attempted to come with me but was waved back. Double shit. Straight to the speech marks.

"Todd's fucked up! He set up some companies and did the IT stuff but he has really messed up."

"How? Why?"

"His last job was to arrange some cash to be transported from NYC to Munich which was then to be moved around Europe." Those bloody criminals and their love of cash. Blondie drew breath and then dropped the bombshell. "He fucked up the flight details; once again, he fucked up the flight details."

The cash was now the property of the German government and Miguel was mad as hell! In the crazy world of the Colombian Cali Cartel it was a drop in the ocean. Heartbreakingly, that could well be the fate of The Todd. Time out. I did not want to appear glib. Two things that will trouble me to the end of my time. Anne and Todd. In prison some social worker tells you that there is always a victim to a crime – they are right. I feel the need to apologise for the tone of the text at times but it is the only way I know. Oh Anne, so sorry, you deserved so much more. Still miss you, still love you.

Then there is Todd, just a dreamer whose dream became a nightmare. Glad the last time I saw him he seemed free; he was laughing and looking forward to the last lap and finally freedom. This was not what it had been all about; guess the gleam and the glamour had dirt under its fingernails and then some.

You miserable selfish shit, Simon. Sorry, Todd.

Back to Geert, who was now wiping away a tear. He knew what would happen, so did I.

We still all had dinner and we all vowed to get out now, while we can. A toast to Todd.

Another sleepless night for me. So pleased to see Geert, Stomp, Mr Tromp, Cruyff, Blondie, Erasmus, and Frans in the morning. I needed them all. We both drank our coffee in silence.

"What next, my friend?"

"Sorry?"

It had been a reassuring silence so I was surprised when it was broken. What next was a good question. We had come out the other side cash rich but we had lost some of ourselves along the way.

Geert repeated the question. This time I managed an answer, saying I was going to try again with Anne. He smiled; oh joy. He told me that Carmen was coming over to Holland; he hoped she would stay. Could not help myself and suggested we all get together for dinner sometime. It was good to laugh a little. Too depressed to go into full details so will get to the point for once. Anne was a no-go. She did not want me back under any terms or in any way. Our dance and our day was done.

I admired her more when she declined any financial help, the house, or any other cash enticements. All I could do was wish her well and offer her a drop-all deal if she ever changed her mind. Blondie had been in contact a few times and he had a similar tale to tell with regard to Carmen Camilla Lopez; bet she was not as polite as Anne. He invited me over to the Netherlands to cheer me up. Why not? Before I left I resigned for good from the bank. The details do not matter except boy were they pissed off.

Boarding a flight again, back to Amsterdam. On arrival there was no time to people watch. Blondie was there waiting, smile beaming. He got it in first, saying it was good to see me. On a small note, on the way out of the airport car park he got extremely close to the car in front which was waiting at the barrier. When the barrier lifted and the car moved he accelerated and we screeched out of the airport. Colour me confused. There was always a line, always an explanation. He said, "Told you I loved crime." He then added that we had just made some more money together. Boy, do you have to laugh.

This ensured the car journey was a merry one, with relationship demons put aside for now.

The only strange thing was that we were driving away from the city. A chuckle, a grin, and, "We are off to the beach, my friend." Had to laugh again. Told you once, told you twice, the man is top company. Oh we do like to be beside the seaside.

Know you'd love a briefcase update. I had left it in a locker at the airport. It was the 90s so not the same security. Took some cash out as I like to pay my way, even if Geert rarely allows this. I need to offer. Onwards and upwards.

We were heading to a coastal town called

Noordwijk – a delightful resort south of Amsterdam. It compares very well with Deauville and if it were a stick of rock it would have class running through it. It has managed to stay off the tourist radar no doubt due to the dubious climate. Though we were slap-bang in the middle of summer, the sky was overcast and the rain hung around in the distance waiting to strike at a moment's notice. It was not dampening our mood though, we may or may not have been singing to the radio as we swept into town.

Sorry to bang on about this but it really is a top town – give it a go sometime. The only odd thing was that we drove past the very fine hotels where according to Geert the Dutch national team rest and recuperate between internationals.

"Oh come on, Blondie. Where are we off to now?"

A smile, then, "My mother's."

Ah, Mrs T. She had a splendid abode by the beach where you could look out over the windswept sands and relax. Bless her, she cooked for us, called us both good boys underneath, and lifted our spirits no end. Without wanting to freak you out, it was nice to be around a warm caring woman again. It was a good period of rest and recuperation for Geert and I. There was no itinerary, no plan and you could do your own thing as long as you made dinner. It was great.

I did not exactly lose track of time but it could have been the 3rd or 4th day when Ma Tromp asked me to take her dog out as it would give me time to think. It was a good idea. She had a lovely loyal black Labrador that had taken a liking to me. It was bliss; the dog ran around at will and I enjoyed the solitude of the sands. Now think. What next? Start a business? Nah, work, staff and ungrateful moaning customers. Travel? Maybe, still a few places I'd like to see. Buy some property? Could do, good to look around, plot, scheme, get a pool and sea view. Shag around? Not that easy; not bad looking and have cash to flash, but not really a ladies' man and still not over Anne. Drink, drugs, and party? No thanks, not that into a life of debauchery. At least I can do any or all of these things and more, so I was somewhat cheered.

My therapy, if that's what you want to call it, was complete when we drove in to Den Hague and hit the casino. House nil, Simon and Geert two. We were both sad to leave – at least we had a lunch with the G-men, so all in all a great few days. I thanked Mrs Tromp and she reiterated her 'good boy' theme and the dog looked devastated to see me leave. It warmed my heart to see Geert and his mum; he was a good boy too. Our smiles were as broad as the beach on the way out of town. So we are both calm and reasonably relaxed, optimistic about the future and as happy as two men can be in the mess of our own making. If you have read any of this and managed to retain it you know that bad news is about to come a-knocking. Oh yes, it is just around the corner waiting to jump out and punch us both!

We had booked lunch at the De Kas restaurant. You eat in a greenhouse – the food served is home grown and made. Google was not around then but search now and then go. A strange but not an unpleasant experience. Vinny and HB were waiting for us so just Jan to come. Wish he hadn't, not that he is not a great guy, but guess who was with him?

Carmen? Not bad but no. Maria? No. Anne? I wish. My ex-boss? Interesting, but why? So no. Mrs Tromp's dog? Now I am just being stupid. Had enough? Yes, me too. It was Miguel. Number one or two in the Columbia Cali Cartel Gentlemen. Fuck, now what?

None of us spoke or greeted him so he got straight to the point. "Judging by the quality of your silence, I assume you assume Todd will not be joining us." Cold. "I am afraid he won't." He then went to explain that he admired our sophistication and culture, however, Colombia was a different world. It was not an excuse as he was not looking to be forgiven; he did or had done what was expected. That was the cold hard fact that he was not trying to hide. He looked at Geert and asked if it would be okay to join us for lunch. He in turn looked to us all for a silent yes or no. Would you stay and have lunch with Miguel? Again, feel the need to apologise for the tone of the text. Have tried my best to be solemn when required but it is written by a man who thinks it is funny to say, "It is hot in here," at a crematorium when attending funerals.

All I can add is that I am not looking for an excuse. I liked Todd. In many ways it was like looking in a mirror. We are both flawed and after a quick fix at best we were prepared to bend the rules to get what we wanted. You could argue that there was no desire to get our hands dirty but hopefully you do not view us as unredeemable individuals. The worrying thing is that I did not dislike Miguel. Call me a snob, as I had total disdain for the gold chain wearing, bickering buffoons in his employ, so it could be that he walked and talked like one of us. He had not tried to hide who or what he was, so I was under no delusions of what he was capable of. At least he paid for lunch in cash, though not red.

It does not help me to say that after some discomfort the conversation was in no way stifled. Time to find out why he had come. You would think as effete snobs using famous painter's names we would have laughed when he told us he admired our work. Another time and circumstance, but then it may have never come up. Anyway, he waxed lyrical about Geert's work in Panama and the rest of the G-men's assistance in the cash movements in Europe. Finally there was praise for my efforts, with his man in the First Inter Americas bank deeply impressed by me. "So, Dutch and English men, I have come here to seek further assistance."

Oh fuck, again and again. Here we go again, to quote Todd and possibly Al – we were out, now could be dragged back in.

CHAPTER 18

Favours are free so let us be!

Miguel stated that we did not owe him or his group anything, good to know. He was Impressed that none of us had asked to be paid and had done it as a favour and for goodwill.

Alright, so we were not expected to respond favourably to the next request. Which is?

He needed some assistance moving hard and electronic cash for his American and Russian friends. He would especially like to help some group or other in New York, not hard to know who. He also stated that it is always a good idea to keep the unpredictable Russians sweet. This just keeps getting worse. Speaking of Todd, his departure had left them without any experienced financial know-how and had lost his contacts as well. Fair play goes to Geert as he did question the decision to kill him, stressing the word 'kill'. Miguel did not shy away from an answer, telling him in many ways that he was right and it was regrettable but that was the way things were done, as it was not quite him or me but it would have weakened his position a great deal not to do it. The problem was, Todd had not only moved cash on the computer, he was also adept at buying and taking over cash-poor companies and establishing cash-fluid businesses. There was no one in Cali and they did not trust any of the proposed alternatives from the US, and they would not leave a gold fish with the Russians, let alone cash.

They had worked with the G-men on many straight deals and had always admired their honesty and valued the contacts they had set up for them in the Netherlands. Geert also spoke Russian and had served as a very competent consultant in the past. All in all they respected their class, which is far more permanent than asking for cash. No word of me yet, you know it is coming. He unfortunately did come round to me. If the Dutch trusted me that was enough; he had also been very impressed with my recent work and that bloody bloke in Panama had not stopped going on about me. It also turns out the pretty waitress from the hotel in Cali was a distant relative who had told a friend of a friend what a true gent I was and how charming I had been. Bloody hell fire! I dug around a little and found some courage.

Have to go around the houses first. First, I thanked him for his words and the compliments and expressed my admiration for him and his group, telling him that we had all treated it as a business transaction and had been impressed with their professionalism. Hollow words but had to sit on my left arm to avoid showing nerves. So, I pressed on with the platitudes, and asked him to pass on my gratitude and send my regards to his man in Panama and to say hello to his relative. Finally, my point was, what if any of us made a mistake? There was no reply. Miguel just stretched his palms out. One testicle had dropped so I continued by explaining that he was not exactly offering us a great deal after poor Todd's treatment. There were no completely risk-free deals and I was pretty sure that he could not guarantee our safety if someone dropped the ball, therefore why would we want to participate in this particular project?

"Money." He explained we could name our price, more or less saying he would go up to 40% on electronic transactions of ten million or more, of which there would be quite a few. With regards to actual cash, it would be 50/50 on every deal. None of us spoke, which troubled him; he wrongly assumed that we were worried that a notoriously tight operation cash-wise was suddenly giving very favourable terms. The explanation was that they would still be making a good profit but the goodwill would last them a lot longer than the cash and cement their business relationships with the Yanks and the Russians. Still nothing, so he started talking telephone numbers for all of us. I had not been proud of much recently but my spirits lifted when there was a collective shrug. Praise was the next tactic. Apparently he wished he could work with us all the time, what class not to be wowed by money. If only his staff thought the same way.

We thanked him but not with any great enthusiasm. He then tried the health and safety card by pledging that if there was a mistake we would not be blamed. He did not believe that himself.

It appeared that Miguel may have played his last

card and Jan and Vinny had thanked him for the kind offer but both said we all needed a break. Even the silent Bosh had passed. That left Blondie to wind things up and send him on his way with no slight given or taken. He was just drawing breath when Miguel played his ace. "By the way, on an unrelated topic, I had dinner with Carmen and her sister the other day and told them I was coming to Europe."

Oh no. All of us except Blondie were doing our utmost to stifle a groan. Frans' fangs were out, those pearly whites were dazzling. He had gone totally gaga; you could see the love light in his eyes. That bloody woman. Would have said, "Well played," to Miguel but I was busy rolling my eyes with the rest of the G-men. All of that rolling was making my eyes tired so I closed them and mentally took myself back to the beach in Holland. What next? Start a business? Nah, work, staff, and ungrateful moaning customers. Travel? Maybe, still a few places I'd like to see. Buy some property? Could do, good to look around plot, scheme, get a pool and sea view. Shag around? Not that easy, not bad looking and have cash to flash, but not really a ladies' man and still not over Anne. Drink, drugs, and party? No thanks, not that into a life of debauchery. At least I can do any or all of these things and more so, somewhat cheered.

Can you see anything about going back to crime? Thought not. I was fed up to the back teeth of the deception, the fear, and just wanted a chance to get my life back on track. It was exciting when it was low-level and I had to admit the flash hotels, good food, and glamour was great.

However, it is not worth dying for. Geert had

regained some composure and had managed to get some words out at last. He told Miguel that none of us were over keen to get involved again so soon and though he did understand the cultural differences, what had happened to Todd had hit a nerve and it was still raw. He spelled out slowly how much money we had moved for free, so they owed us. Our South American colleague nodded his agreement at all of these points and suggested we meet for dinner where he would have a detailed plan and we could talk it over together. Again, it was highlighted that we were under no obligation to assist the CCCG. Once again my client relationship manager side kicked in, offering him coffee and asking if he wanted showing round town. His smile was of the sinister nature but he kindly refused, explaining that he had some other people to see that afternoon who had been introduced to him thanks to the G.

Geert and I accompanied him to the door where Blondie gave him a pay as you go mobile which he always had in his possession, telling him he would send him details of the restaurant. He then apologised to me and asked if I minded leaving him and his friends alone for an hour or so. I agreed with a pat on the back and told him to take as long as they needed. He gave me a mobile and said he'd send me a text with the time and place of the planned meeting point. It was 3pm. Even though Geert had just an hour I did not plan to re-join the G-men till dinner. Therefore there was about three or four hours to fill.

Best not use 'kill'. The urge to run was my first thought. I had the money and sadly had no one so could just keep running. This whole business had ended twice. The first was a happy occasion, I had everything a man my age needed – financial freedom, a beautiful loving wife, property, and complete carte blanche to do what I wanted and go where I wanted. The second occasion, though far more melancholic had still felt like the end. I had lost the love but was cautiously optimistic. Now there was this mess. There would be no fun, only fear.

There may be money but it could come with the ultimate cost. I liked Vinny, Jan, and Bosh but like me they looked like they had had enough. So all that was left was mine and their loyalty to Geert. The question was, how far any of us were prepared to go to show it. He had sounded quite convincing at the end of lunch, but where Carmen was concerned who knew what his instinct would tell him? Although he was far from faithful, he did have a son with her; that bonded them and Blondie appeared to be addicted to her unpredictability. So he could well decide to agree to help Miguel and do his bidding for him. To be honest, as much as I liked and even admired Geert, I had absolutely no desire to carry on further with this caper. Run, Simon. Run.

Once again it looked like there was going to be a personal battle with my conscience. My parents especially my father would kill me if I ran. They might not be the only ones. My dad had never run away from anything in his life and while it might be easy to admire Geert, my dad was a hero. He was everything a man should be. Honest, loyal, and he would take any job and do anything to support and defend his family. He never complained and was completely selfless when it came to his wife and family. If only I could be more like him. He had told me many times, whatever situation you get yourself in you have to find a way out. Always finish what you start and never forget your family will always be there for you. Maybe should give him a call; he would simply tell Miguel to do one, no fear.

So, looks like I will be wandering around Amsterdam in a daze again. Haven't we been here before? After two hours walking I found a quiet café by a canal with an outside terrace, ordered coffee and just stared at the water hoping for some sort of soothing effect. No chance; the brick-like object in my pocket was buzzing and vibrating away, not an unpleasant experience as it goes. There was no caller ID back in the day so I debated whether to answer, but in truth it could only be one person calling. There is no need to type the name as you know too. So I answered. Blondie did not bother with any small talk, he just asked where I was. He knew the café and said he would be along shortly. The bloody canal was less than useless; there was no soothing effect at all. May as well have another coffee and stare into space.

We have hit a bit of a wall here. Where do we go next? Oh, back in the beginning this tome was full of hope advertising forthcoming trips, sneaking about, making cash. The only thing the cash was making me now was sick. That may sound silly but I'd now had enough – so full.

Before these thoughts could fester Blondie was sat next to me also staring into space. I was not surprised when the first coherent thing he said to me was that it was just him and me now. There was no bitterness and he went on to explain that he had told his friend that they did not need to agree to anything. In fact, he would prefer it if they didn't. His instructions were for them to get out now and go and get some sun and relax. The G-men protested but to no avail. They were out. "What shall we do, my friend? Because I don't know what to think and what to do anymore." It was a good question and I was not sure of the answer myself, so shrugged.

Blondie then shrugged; what a pair we made. Rich beyond the dreams of the normal man, free to go where we wanted, but ultimately fucked. In the end it was my idea to go and meet Miguel and at least hear what he had in mind. What a pair of wankers, how stupid can you get? Even though we could be about to walk through the darkest valley, fear no evil, for you are with us; your rod and your staff, they comfort me. So please bear with us on this. Let us mix up Voltaire's maxim to 'you may disapprove of what we are about to do but we will defend to the death your right to disapprove'.

We both started laughing at the absurdity of our position. Damned if we do, maybe dead if we don't. It was enough to put you off your food; not the best timing as we had dinner plans.

Miguel did not look at all surprised when just the two of us pitched up for dinner and rather annoyingly said that he assumed the others would not be joining him and us. Smug git. God bless Geert; he fired back with the fact that they had better things to do, but this still did not ruffle our Colombian friend's feathers and he just added, "Shall we?"

Blondie wasn't finished though, and told Miguel that were not hungry and maybe we could just have a drink and it would be good if he could get to the point as we had other plans. May have seen a little frown appear, but there was just a fine! So, off to the bar we went. I ordered three tonic waters, much to Geert's amusement and Miguel's surprise. Sod him. He thanked us for coming and passed on Carmen's best wishes to her husband, and added how pleased she was that he was helping her friends. The bastard then knifed my friend in the heart by telling him what a beautiful, intelligent son they had together. Miguel may dress to impress and have European cultural sensitivities but he was a cold, calculating man to his core.

My turn to step up, and I said to him that we were not present to discuss happy families and pressed him to disclose his plan. It was almost identical to the last time they had asked for help. They needed Geert to wave his wand and move cash from country to country. My job was Todd's old one, more or less. As I now came highly recommended they would like me to go to New York and advise his new best friends on electronic transfers and potential business for their dough. Again, he was talking telephone numbers and seemed to think being held in high esteem by his group and other associates would give us a thrill. It just gave me a chill.

Before I replied to the plan I looked over at Geert to see if there was any inkling of how he was and what he was thinking. Nah, cool as, as always. Okay. Told the big Mig that the plan was possible but the money was neither here nor there. My own reservation was that the people who we were helping had an unsavoury reputation and I had no desire to fraternise with them, meet them, or to be honest, help them. Not a flicker.

Blondie's turn. He asked Miguel why he needed our help and why he wanted to aid Gringos. Could it be he was in trouble? A flicker. Ha. That blow had drawn blood. He was clearly flustered. He started rambling on about being a businessman and wanting to help the Cali community, and only wanted the best for his country. What total and utter bullshit.

We had reached an impasse. There was now an extremely uncomfortable silence which no one seemed to want to break. It was a little like the graveyard seen in The Good, The Bad and The Ugly. Boom, boom, be, boom. Ding, ding.

Miguel fired first. "Dutchman, think of the financial freedom you will be giving your young, beautiful family. They will be set up for life."

Not bad, but Blondie fired back, saying his family had enough. He then called a ceasefire by saying we would both give it some more thought and contact him tomorrow. He promised a yes or no answer. Miguel nodded his acceptance. Like to think we left with a slight advantage when Geert mentioned we had to meet some very important and influential people that evening who we had agreed to help. Then slam dunked it with a smile. It was not reciprocated and was only met with a frown, so I winked at him. We patted each other on the back simultaneously outside and laughed our balls off. At least we ended the day on the high. We both agreed not to discuss it further until the following morning. Why spoil the moment? Anyway, there would soon be another sleepless night to worry. Till then, a small victory to savour and a chance of salvation and maybe we could get out of this yet.

The morning arrived. It seemed strange, almost out of place. Though did remind me of the dreams I had been chasing so I think it will be possible to make this pay. These day, these days. Can take care of all of this and use outward deception to get away. After all, it is a modern age. So please stay for these days. Wonder if I can just keep repeating myself?

Blondie and I met at the same café where he gave me the brown paper bag full of cash. He was a big fan of irony for a clogster and once again arrived with a full brown bag. No money, only bread, but still funny. So the morning started as the previous day had finished. If we do not help the Machiavellian Miguel, our story ends here. Sure we have done this before as well. Fuck it, I wish it had. You should know me by now or you will never, never, never know me at all. Simply red-faced about that. At this point in my life, though my circle of friends was quite small, they were good ones. But did any of them know who I had become? At least my friend Geert knew me warts and all, so if he wanted to do it, I would. When his first sentence was his worry about the safety of his son, I knew we were in. Oh well, stop dreaming of the quiet life.

On an unrelated note: Thank you for your submission but I'm afraid I didn't love this enough to want to pursue it further. Best wishes.

Well, you are entitled to your opinion. Just to show there are no hard feelings, please let me get you a coffee and help yourself to some of Blondie's bread.

Bye for now; we are off on our travels again. Rather than book some elaborate dinner venue, Geert asked Miguel to meet us in a traditional Dutch pancake house. We sat on long bench-like tables surrounded by a young hip crowd. The food was great, almost as good as the discomfort Miguel clearly felt judging by his expression. He was the only person in a suit which had not gone unnoticed and was been openly mocked. Told you that man Geert has style. Another small victory, though maybe hollow.

CHAPTER 19

Start spreading the news,

we are off today.

I was off to New York the following day and Blondie was off to Colombia. We shared the first part of the leg together, as sticking to the code, we were off to Toronto.

It was not planned but we decided to have a night out on the town in Toronto. It was a blast. Close again, those Canadian ladies sure like the English. This amused us both so much so that Blondie forgot to flirt and we went back to the hotel together. Blimey, whatever next?

Sadly that was the end of our time together for a while. He was off to sort through the Cali cash deposits. Told him I hoped to see him soon. BIG smile. Start spreading the news, it is my time to be part of New York. Oh, joy. No more flights at least, I have a nice long drive – eight hours or more. Before finally agreeing to any of this I had insisted on dealing with as few people as possible and had also said I did not want to socialise. I told Miguel to keep it as formal as possible and that it was to be purely business. Less is more, being the motto. Thankfully it appeared he had kept his word.

My hotel was a most boutique one but had a certain class. The room was good and the dining areas had a touch of style. The obligatory phone was waiting for me with a number to call pre-saved. The man who answered seemed civil enough and a meeting was arranged in a small coffee shop close to my hotel. So far so good. Sure there is no need for a tour of NYC so let's skip it and get to the meeting. Once again, promises had been met with just two business, not track-suited gentlemen sent to meet me. There was also not a gold chain in sight.

They were amiable enough and no names were given or asked – okay. We got straight into it. I asked them what they needed and they told me; good, simple business. Oh, you would like to know? Not too much to it, but alright. They wanted me to meet their banker and just go over what he was doing and show him how to set up some dummy corporations and explain what exactly me and the G-men had worked out for Miguel and his mates. Quite low level and low risk. It seemed they weren't asking me to do any actual transfers or make any arrangements so I was happy enough. The next topic of conversation was their cash flow situation. They had it coming in from all manner of sources which mercifully they did not go into too much detail about.

Sure you can guess what type of business they were operating. Just watch any of the stereotypical Italian American films then make them an offer they cannot refuse. There were bars, there were cars, and still rivers of cash. The problem, if you can call it that, there was simply too much cash. They had bought businesses and financed some schemes or other but their money worries came from the fact that they could not process it properly and lived in fear, again, if that is the right word, of the IRS, FBI, or some other agency getting their hands on it.

For such a large organisation they were remarkably small where business was concerned. I explained to them that unlike Todd I did not exactly have my finger on the pulse of cash business Stateside, but did have a few suggestions. They nodded for me to continue. I started with just one word – franchise – which again got a nod to elaborate. I explained the basic principles in the least condescending way possible, then got to the main crux of it and ran a few names past them (hopefully you know the usual suspects as I cannot afford any lawsuit or pay a copyright). You pay a chunk of change to get the name; the bigger the name the higher the price. Then you pay a percentage of your profits. A big nod. Wow, must be impressed. Told them I could do the groundwork on this and then turn it over for them to sign the contracts and let the cash run free to the other side. A thumbs-up, good to go then. Feeling good, I thought, *Fuck it*, and said, "Football."

"What, buy the Giants or the Jets?"

Ah. "Soccer."

"You mean gay football." This did come with a smile.

I told them to buy a soccer franchise. After the

glory years of the early 70s the Yanks were about to give football another try, with the MLS planning to kick off again. This time they did speak and asked for more details. So I laid out a scenario – buy a part-time club. After some investment bid to be a part of the league. Find a 15-20k arena, rent or lease long-term, all cash-paying customers, guess you will have 'house full' signs every game. This drew a laugh and a smattering of applause and the regulatory pat on the back.

May as well pat myself on the back while I am here. They told me they had heard I was good and now increased the adjective to say I was great. Oh, gee, thanks guys. I didn't say that, hence the lack of speech marks; just a cool nod. They asked me to do the donkey work, find a club, indoor arena, and look at what the MLS wanted. Still feeling good, I asked them who the invoice should be addressed to and where to send it. Got a 'nice one, Limey' for that particular gem. All in all, a very agreeable and successful meeting.

They asked me to update them in a week, same time and place. If you are still with us you know this text has no imagination and lacks originality, so let's say that everything was done and everyone was happy. However, you know that there may be trouble ahead, why else would something positive be included? The first downturn was the banker. For those outside the UK, (fingers crossed, aim high) it is used to rhyme with wanker. Actually that is way too weak, would need to add 'total and utter' to even get close to describe him.

His nose had clearly been put out of joint with my inclusion as he seemed to resent me breathing the same air as him and was not backwards in coming forwards when showing contempt for my mere being. When I took him through what I considered to be the best ways of money transfer and setting up safe heavens and accounts with no identity, at best he tolerated my suggestions. All he kept saying was that he could have come up with that as it was too simple. I tried to explain using the 'less is more' approach but he was intent on the need to dazzle and delude with his deals. He openly said to my face that he could not believe that he had to listen to the Sesame Street guide to finance from a Limey. He then went on a minor rant of 'do you know who I am?' This was followed by a list of people whose names were dropped in some sort of fruitless intimidation tactic. The man was begging for a bullet to the head. He saw himself as one of New York's masters of the universe, striding the global market and living the high life. The man was a fraud through and through. I checked him out before our meeting and grade-wise, bank-wise and client portfolio-wise, he was nothing.

Wish someone would tell him this, though I am not sure the facts would get in the way of his ego. I'd had enough of his attitude so told him my job was done I and was only doing a friend a favour. Then explained that I would inform (good phrase to throw around) my contacts of his attitude and reluctance to listen. This was like a red rag to a bull. He went off on one; he demanded to know who my contacts were and then listed everyone from Al Capone to Marlon Brando as people he could call on in his words to do me in. Think he may have said 'whack', not 'do me in', but I hope you catch me, or should that be 'my meaning'?

Anyway, no handshake was offered, so I simply shrugged and left the most important man in Manhattan to it. Should have left him a spade but I'm sure the irony would have been missed.

At the next meeting with the mystery men I reported in the most diplomatic way possible that I had found their guy less than wise and was more than happy to wash my hands of him and any further deals or advice. The nodding was back so it seemed they did not wish to hear any more. They did thank me for my efforts and I felt slightly more reassured when the pat on the back was back.

The rest of the day and evening lay ahead. I was not in the mood to eat alone and did not fancy a drink, and even though I am reliably informed that finding a woman is like fishing in a barrel with dynamite for an Englishman in New York, I settled for a walk and took in some of the sights and sounds of the city. There was, or there were, worse things to do and worse places to be, so not a bad way to spend my time. Back at my hotel there was another mobile phone waiting for me. Blimey, those crims loved them almost as much as cash. It rang shortly after and I was cheered to chat to Blondie. A sane voice in an insane situation. He laughed at my day and on hearing about his, it was my turn. All of his suggestions, though sound, had resulted in full-blown argument with the various other parties.

They were bickering over every dollar bill and testing his patience to the max. Talk about an early rendition of Mad Men; absolutely nothing to do with advertising but I hope you get my premise. Another sleepless night for me.

The situation got worse the following morning when I literally bumped into M&M in the lobby. Not that one, Machiavellian Miguel. Come on, keep up. When will it end? There did not appear to be any immediate danger as he was over the top in his greeting and ushered me into the lounge for coffee. I hoped this may be the worst thing to happen today. I contemplated the diplomatic approach, however, I was weary of all the bullshit and for once took the moral high ground and got straight to the point. Asked what he wanted and told him to make it quick as it was time for me to go home. He was in no way perturbed by my tone and actually apologised for the banker and the lack of respect he had shown me. Oh. I did not like where this could go. I told him that no offense was taken and asked again what he wanted.

"You are very direct this morning, Englishman. Are you sure you are not upset?"

I assured him I was happy as a man in my situation could be, which did bring a smile. Maybe I should have ordered a spade for myself as Café Man One and Two thought I was great. Well, we know that they told me to my face. Therefore the banker was out and though it was not put that way, if I wanted to be out they would like me to move the money through cyberspace for them. Talk about digging a bloody gapping great big hole.

Just for a moment, I thought I had found a way. Now, as destiny unfolded, it looked like I was here to stay for a while longer. At that moment my mobile buzzed with a message from Blondie. it read, 'sorry my friend, if it helps they need me for a while longer.' I laughed despite myself.

This threw the big M enough to start thanking me for heaven knows what. Had to shut him up and asked if my best friend the banker would be receiving a financial settlement. He actually blushed and assured me he was alive and would not be harmed unless I deemed it necessary. I've got the power. Sorry to say it was quite tempting. Nah, don't go there, Simon. Leave him. Sure karma will catch up with him, at least it will divert it from Geert and me. I managed to keep my head down and do the deals and then had all the facts on the football.

I prayed that there would not be a replay or any time added on. Told anyone who had asked that I didn't have time to socialise but thought it prudent to have at least one dinner to fill them in on the football and answer any questions, even got hold of Geert who was going to fly in. Miguel had booked the Oak room in the Plaza so at least we'd have a classy evening and fine food to look forward to, hopefully. Blondie baulked at my hotel and insisted we check in to the Plaza which may give us some advantage, and the man only did five star. He was in a fine mood considering the current circumstances. He had spent quite a bit of time with young Johan and Carmen had told him he was the man. I repeated this last part quizzically and told him it just sounded like a normal Dutch family name. From now on he could call himself Geert de Man but was a little worried about Carmen de Man. Quite rightly, he roared with laughter and we headed for dinner in a happy frame of mind. In the lift, or shall we use elevator as we are in the USA, he asked me about our cut. I told him not to worry as I had set up a ghost company in the Cayman Isles whose cash we would both have access to.

I had been totally transparent with this, informing all who needed to know. Big smile. There were six of us for dinner; the two men with no names, plus a new man with no name. Miguel, Blondie, a man with many names, and me. The three mystery men and Miguel toasted us and were fulsome with their praise for our efforts. I had prepared a glossy handout about my football plans and had lined up plenty of people on the inside for them to consult, work with, or bribe. Hoped it was not going to be my problem. This was also well received all that was left was to enjoy dinner then get out of there. The food was very fine indeed and the conversation was light and enjoyable. The only strange thing was the Yanks' attitude to Miguel. Far from respecting him, they tried to belittle him when possible and openly mocked his choice of wine. If you are a film aficionado you would expect a reaction and a scene.

Far from it; he took it and took it some more. What the hell? Geert looked puzzled as he had picked up on it too. At one point when he was talking they interrupted him and asked our opinion on a completely unrelated topic. There was the odd twitch here and there but he did not take the bait. It was odd to say the least, and apart from wanting the meal to be over as soon as possible, the thought crossed my mind that Mrs T. and her sadistic sister should be here to observe his treatment. Geert would definitely be Geert De Big Man then and forever.

Thankfully the meal ended without any further incident, as I did my David Niven and Geert did his Rutger Hauer and his Blondie, his Frans, Erasmus, and a Cruyff for dessert. Our old world charm had gone down well, with us even getting a laugh by promising to come back and run the city for them. After all, it was New Amsterdam before it became New York.

Who knows or understands the scheme of things? In his world, Miguel was feted and swooned over, and remember someone even curtsied. His reputation got things done where here he was just about being tolerated, best not to ask why. They liked Blondie and me. So much so that when the cheque came they asked Miguel to pick it up and asked us to join them for a nightcap sans a now unhappy-looking Columbian. We adjourned to the Rose Club where once again unironically rose a glass to our contribution business and dinner. This time the glass was filled with Louis XIII brandy. Not a bad drop if I do say myself. Are we there yet?

The end!

If you are still with us you know this text has no imagination and lacks originality, so let's say this is not the end. You know that there may be trouble ahead. What else do you expect by now? There was one final funny moment when they gave Geert a metallic briefcase, no doubt stuffed with cash. The funny part was that they hoped he liked the stuff as much as them. Hell yeah! It came at a cost, of course. There was a final favour. Fucking final favour may serve as my epitaph. Could we sort the Reds under the beds out? So many jokes about maids and hotels but to help, a clearly confused-looking Blondie asked how we could possibly help the Ruskies.

Well, they had heard the Dutchman spoke Russian and could use his help with some discussion or other.

To get them to the table, in their words, they would like me to press some buttons to send them some money. Even though we were in the Hotel Plaza and not California we could check out but could not leave yet. We politely refused the offer of a night on the town. Who needs all that? It was not taken the wrong way and there were handshakes all round in the bar. The Russians would be coming in two days. Great.

Before leaving, the Americans had insisted our stay in the Plaza was on them. Quite a generous gesture given the setting. Geert ordered two more brandies; may as well, as they are free. He did not seem overly stressed, mind you he never did. His words were, "This is the last one, I promise." I almost believed him. Blondie was also quite happy for another reason. Miguel had been mocked in front of us, which would be useful ammunition should we need it. Sure the sycophantic following in Cali might be interested to know about this.

He was not worried about repercussions from the muted Mig as we were in with the New York crew who he feared. Almost happy days. He wasn't finished with the positives. Due to the fact his new name was De Man, his doting spouse had agreed to let his son stay with his angelic mother for a few months. He hoped to make this move permanent but you had to be careful with the cunning Carmen Camila Lopez. I was very happy for my friend and for me, as if he was trying to move his son to Europe this may be the last one. Though we had refused to spend the rest of the evening with our dinner companions, the brandy and optimistic feeling gave us a boost so we hit the town.

I would dearly like to give you a full account but the details are still a bit hazy even now. The basic facts are: Geert took a fair chunk of change from the case. There was none left by the morning. I did wake up alone, which was fine, but Blondie brought two blondes to breakfast. Sure they were lovely, however, I was so hungover could only apologise and go back to bed. It must have been lunch time when my bedside phone rudely interrupted my slumber. Sorry, America, but sometimes your accent can feel like inserting a drill in your ear. In your defence it may have been the hangover, or the news the receptionist gave me. There were two gentlemen waiting for me in the lobby who wished to speak to me. Would sooner take my chances with Blondies blondes.

A swift shit, shower, and a shave and I made my way to see who the mystery men were, though we all know. Sure enough, it was One and Two. They had some account information and wanted me to do a transfer. Explained I would need a bank to do this. They and you may wonder how the last ones were done. I told them that I had some contacts in NYC who had let me use their offices and had allowed me to access my own and other networks. However, that took time and planning and I would not be able to arrange it that afternoon. They did not seem that put out and asked if there was any other way. Oh, karma, my friend, thank you for sparing me for now. "Well, how about your banker? Sure if you came with me he would let us use his system."

They started laughing, saying I had style and, said, "I am sure he will!" So off we went.

The G-men may call me Rembrandt, but I would

still struggle to paint a picture of our friendly banker's face when we arrived unannounced. I still had no idea who the men I was with were but he clearly did. Colour – anaemic white. Demeanour – bricking it. Temperature – hot and sweaty. Art work he most resembled – The Scream. Ha bloody ha.

My new best buddies were brutal in their instructions. While my ear may not always be able to take the accent, I love the Yanks' ability to cut the crap and cut to the chase. Speaking of which, they told him if he didn't help they would cut his balls off and if the Englishman was not happy (that's me) they would come back and cut his tiny dick off. Finally my smile may have reached Geert-like levels. He was then instructed to get us coffee and then get the fuck out of here until he was told to come crawling back. It was my turn to tell them how much I admired their style. More laughter.

The transaction was easy and didn't take long. However, when I showed One and Two the magic of technology there was a few back slaps and some sort of high five. Just to make the day complete they played the hooky-cokey (pokey) with our now bashful banker. In, out, and do believe he did the shaking about. This time he did shake my hand on departure and offered his help 24/7. Believe the boys told him to save it for losers like him. That was my work done and I was planning a rest day until my new finance gurus insisted I came along for the ride to watch them stick it to the Ruskies. Knew there had to be some bad news hanging around somewhere. When I got back to the hotel Geert seconded this request. Da.

What the hell they needed me for, lord alone

SIMON CARROLL

knows. This became even clearer when all parties in this particular negotiation had manned up.

In the North American corner they had beefed up their security metaphorically and literally. In the South American corner there was beef but closer to the bone. In the Russian corner Ray Ban had had a good day as there were no eyeballs to be seen. Finally, in the charming if somewhat misguided European corner, there was me and Blondie. This was amusing him as he described me as his muscle. Now you have history and information at your fingertips, if you are surfing on the Plaza homepage there is plenty of both. Pretty sure our meeting does not feature though. In the hotel's long illustrious past they have hosted the lot. Kings and Queens, Heads of State, Business Giants, and anyone who is anyone in the celebrity world. Deals had been done, truces had been brokered, and mighty corporations formed. Then there was this pumped-up, testosterone-fuelled, testy affair. Three languages were in use and being spoken all at once. Unfortunately for Mr Tromp, he spoke all three so was being called upon at regular intervals to make sense of this mess. My part was trying to rise above the melee and look solemn. Easy enough.

The room resembled the Last Day of Pompeii painting; I just silently hoped there would be no eruptions. After a terminally long time it appeared some sort of deal had been agreed, thank fuck! Champagne arrived; the Russians did not bother with the glasses, drinking from the bottle. Miguel's mob bickered about the brand and the Americans filled their glasses to the brim. We asked for tonic water and had a private toast; we've got to get out of this place. The Russians were not coming, they were now going. Yeah.

Miguel came over, thanked us, and told us if ever we needed his help we only had to call. Then he also did one, no doubt to avoid the indignity of the Americans being disrespectful in front of his posse. Finally, the three mystery men approached our quiet corner. We were both offered full-term membership of their mob, which we somehow manged to avoid without upsetting them. We settled for a similar deal to the one offered by Miguel. We now had an emergency number each. The Yanks thanked us thoroughly and there were pats, hugs, handshakes, and kisses. We had done our job well, both still standing and reputation intact. Now which is the quickest way out?

CHAPTER 20

Sophia and South Africa

Where to next? Easier to give you the lowdown on Geert. He was having his son flown to Holland. A week with his mum then they were all off to South Africa. I did not really have a plan but has we were still in summer, tail end of August if you care, I fancied a relaxing grand tour of Europe; classic car, fine food, some summer sun and a chance to breathe. My French was passable so fancied France. Could change my name to Paul West. Side bar Mr Stephan Clarke, I salute you, bravo.

The Geert guide to international travel was in full swing so we were off to Italy first. One does like to keep ones promises so strap yourself in, it is time for a Rant about Rome.

First things first, it is a toilet, albeit a very old toilet. Rome is dirty and stinks.

Second, our supposed five-star hotel had four – too many. Substandard service, rotten rooms, and plumbing installed in Roman times.

Third, the food. I had dreamed of checked table cloths and simple but fine food. Wrong, the restaurateurs tried to rip you off at every turn. They had reckoned without Geert and me. We may be many things but we knew our reds and laughed at the ridiculous prices they tried to force on us. As for the food, I have eaten better frozen pizzas.

Still ranting. The history was overrated and I nearly dialled my emergency number when we were repeatedly hushed in the Sistine Chapel. I did point out to the self-titled protectors of the painting that it was not theirs and they neither owned it nor painted it. Rome and history, it should stay there. Please don't go.

The only positive to come was the final day when Geert told me he had planned a trip out of town. So keen, I skipped breakfast, but not Italy's only redeeming feature – the coffee. I did not care where we went so my expectations were non-existent but was giddy as a child at Christmas when we arrived at a classic car showroom. May as well call him my best friend now, sure had class. He told me to take my pick. After much deliberation I finally decided on the Ferrari 250 GT Berlinetta Lusso in silver. The graceful curving lines, the elegance and the sheer style completely won me over. Blondie loved the irony of paying for it from his silver briefcase. Hard to be unhappy, but I did give him a friendly lecture on carrying that sort of cash about especially over international borders.

In one ear, out the other. In truth I was not listening to myself as I was too busy admiring the new love of my life. Now, what to call her? It is very important to name your car, people. I decided on

Sophia, after Sophia Loren, another Italian beauty and possibly the same age. We drove back to the eternal city together in Sophia. Blondie was banging on about how he wished he could come on my grand tour. I was just hoping that no irate Italian maniac would bang into my beauty.

Back at the hotel we shared one last coffee before we went our separate ways for a while. Geert had received an email from his son so was happier about his life choices. To help, he painted a picture of his mother and Johan and the dog on the beach together, either Holland or South Africa. It did the trick. He asked me about my plans. Get your map books out, kids. My plan was to drive up the west coast of Italy in my baby. I could pop into Pisa, maybe take a tour around Tuscany. Oh yes, there is Florence as well. Following on from that, France. Maybe Monaco could be nice to see. Nice. Think you get the picture. My goal was to buy some property in the South of France. Time for some recycling before I set off.

Think about the potential house on the beach, easy living, good wine, fine food, long walks, no pressure, and freedom. Breezy but warm nights, the sky is royal blue and I can see all the stars as I lay on a quilt in the lush sand. Everything is calm and I am okay. The only thing missing was holding Anne's hand; guess you cannot have it all, after all. Still, I could call when I get there. You never, never know. This was the best I had felt since San Diego.

Time to say goodbye to Geert. We both became quite emotional. We may deserve to be mocked and certainly not pitied. The choices we made may have been mad, but were our own. At the end of the day we were both still youngish and fucking loaded. Sorry, tone again.

There had been some downs, if it helps. I had lost the love of my life and Geert could still not solve the Carmen conundrum. Still, I am sure you would swop places with us.

All in all we both felt we had made it to the other side and could now follow our dreams. We swore eternal friendship and promised to check in with each other once or twice a month.

Glassy eyed to say the least, let's give over the final words to out multi-named Dutchman.

You may have seen them before.

"Simon, today is the perfect day to start living your dreams. You can fake your way to the table but you have to learn to eat and you have. Simon, my friend, I knew you were our guy. Bye for now." Would it be a stretch to say the sun was just setting as I drove off and Blondie made his way to the airport? Well it was. Trust me, I am a banker.

Wow, this feels like a great place to end. However, that would make the first page irrelevant and why would I tell you that Geert was on his way to South Africa? If it helps I would quite like to end here. For any potential publishers (none to date), how about two books?

You can pay me twice as well while we are at it; you'd better, remember, my emergency phone numbers. Think we all need a little break for now as I do not want to rub your noses in it. There will be very few details about my upcoming trip. I will therefore leave you with some words from Mr Carroll. Don't panic – Lewis, not me. P.S. do we have to pay dead poets?

A boat, beneath a sunny sky

Lingering onward dreamily

In an evening of July*

Long has paled that sunny sky:

Echoes fade and memories die:

Autumn frosts have slain July.

Still she haunts me, phantomwise.

Anne moving under skies

Never seen by waking eyes.

In a Wonderland they lie,

Dreaming as the days go by,

Dreaming as the summers die:

Ever drifting down the stream—

Lingering in the golden gleam—

Life, what is it but a dream?

Haven't we been here before?

*Actually August, do not quibble.

The temperature was 100 degrees Fahrenheit. I stank; my body was running with sweat, my armpits having turned into human fountains. The people there to meet me had insisted on a ban on sunglasses so the glare of the sun was blinding. I am pretty sure many of you at some point in your life have said to yourself, "What the hell am I doing here?" Well, I was standing under an old dilapidated airport hangar somewhere in South Africa at the laughingly titled Upington International airport.

Do you remember this from the beginning of our tale?

Well, we are nearly there, it may be the end. Oh, come on. We know it isn't the start so what is it? Come on then.

After a marvellous month or two driving round Italy and France, just moving my Ferrari and me, all silver and shiny, the sun in my eyes, I missed my buddy but was happy as can be.

It was early October and after a happy house hunt had bought one. Well, it was my birthday. 8th October, if you are interested. So, sat on my terrace overlooking the Med, yep, you guessed it. Time for a text. Go on, you know you and I have to.

Hello my friend hope you are living the dream, know that I am give me a call when you can. Blondie

Like my American friends, I will cut the crap. The flight to South Africa will be boarding very soon. First, the Frans flight guide. Paris to Cairo. Cairo to Riyadh. Riyadh to Nairobi. Dizzy? Me too. Finally, a flight to Cape Town. Stop dreaming of the quiet life. I know I don't, but I feel you miss the madness of other people's money. Here we go again.

Frans was in a festive mood on my arrival and we had long since dropped the cool as façade and we hugged like long-lost brothers. It was great to see him. I knew there would be trouble ahead; still, how long can you sit in the sun in the South of France?

Don't worry, that was rhetorical. We spent the first few days shooting the breeze, reliving past glories and all in all enjoying ourselves. Guess you can't overstate the case for Cape Town. First, there is the beauty of the craggy mountain range, then there's the pristine white beaches lapped by – it must be said – a chilly Atlantic full of sharks. Cape Town has a cool urban edge, excellent art galleries, cool bars, and world-renowned restaurants, so I was not unhappy to be there. Blondie was in his element and very much at home. After all, the Dutch had planted the first gardens and built the sombre Castle of Good Hope in 1666. Sure, the English may have a history down there, but best to skate over that.

By the third day the reason I was here revealed itself. Geert had met some guys. The guys had a lot, and I mean a lot, of cash. They needed it moving. You could not make this up, honest. I have the pictures of the cash somewhere.

So off we go again, the Dutch and Englishman ride again. **You know where we are now**!

I got there first and we were there to meet the soon to be ex-Nigerian Minister of Finance, who was accompanied by several large men with machine guns. Like workmen looking down a hole, we were peering into several crates stuffed with one hundred dollar bills. In total there was close to $500 million. Geert was not far behind me, not sure why we came separately, it is neither here nor there. As soon as he saw all the cash his eyes went all gaga. He was practically salivating at the sight of all the money set out before us. Feel it has become my catchphrase so here it comes. What the hell am I doing here?

One of the minster's flunkies mopped his brow and then offered the same service to Blondie and me. Thankfully not the same hankie. You may wonder why this particular detail is included. Well, it was the highlight of the whole day. The rest was the predictable nonsense you and I have become accustomed to. The cash that looked like it was coming out of the containers, needed to be moved to a safe haven fast. That wasn't all; there was another hangar full of money. I really did not want any part of this in any shape or form. Sadly, the same could not be said for Geert. I could hear his inner monologue cha-chinging. Our esteemed Minister of State reckoned there was $1.2 billion in total. I broke my silence more in shock, to ask how he knew that. Well, the man who mopped brows was also head cash counter. Would you like to hear Geert gasp? Well, just say 20% to him – it does help if it is connected to a large amount of cash, say $1.2 billion. That's $120 million each if we pull it off. Blimey, if we are not careful we will be on one of those rich list lists.

No, still do not want anything to do with this, though I did take the big bag of money they gave me for my troubles. I had to, they were armed to the teeth. Always accept what a man backed up with machine guns gives you, is my motto. Believe we both told them we would need time, to get away and for Blondie to look lovingly at all the lolly. You know I love the man but I was happy we had come separately and also that we had agreed to zig-zag back to his base in Cape Town in separate directions. It would have been crazy to drive but after three connecting flights, not sure either of us saved that much time, so we did not meet up till dinner the following day. By the way, it is about an eight- to ten-hour drive; as we have already upset Rome best move on.

Please lock your doors if you are daring enough to drive, and no valuables, especially bags of cash. Back in Geert's gaffe (he'd also bought a place) he was now the giddy one. All he kept saying was, "Think of all that money, think of all that money." I told him I was but not in the same way as him. It was way, way too much. There was no chance it could be moved.

We agreed to disagree and had a few drinks and dinner. We were both thinking it but I was glad when Blondie said, "My friend, we have come a long way so there is no possibility of falling out over a tiny bit of cash." He sure is De Man.

There was no mention of the money over breakfast but I was sure it could not be far away. To save you the suspense, we did chat about the money again. Blondie also liked to recycle and once again told me that crime was his true love and his real business. It was the buzz, the not knowing, the thrill and trying to stay one step ahead. All easy to understand. His strongest argument was that it made him smile. He flashed a smile and asked if I trusted him. You can't help but smile back. Guess what? Yup, there will be no risk to me. Okay, okay, I made it clear that there was no way I was going back to that airport and did not want to see, touch, or be anywhere near the cash. All fine. However, I did promise to go to Zurich to see what could be done about all those dollars. One more for the road. "Simon, my friend, I knew you were my guy." It appears we were a special kind of business partners. I was his guy and he was de man. What was a man to do? What indeed?

Truth be told there was no hope and I think Blondie knew that too. Even his love of money could not blind him to the fact that deal was all wrong. The location. It was miles from anywhere we knew. The people. We didn't know them and at best their organisation was haphazard. The money. Way too much and all in cash. Think deep down we both realised that I was only going to go through the motions in Zurich and pretty sure Blondie, despite his many talents and ability, could not make that amount of money vanish. When you are right you are right. My contacts in Zurich did not want to know. Must apologise as the use of contacts is stretching it a little. I only spoke to two. One CFO from a large loan company that is a subsidiary of a huge Swiss bank. He enjoyed the conversation and may have even thought about it for a tiny second, but it was way too risky. My other guy, number three in another big Swiss bank and golf partner of the CEO, already had a fleet of luxury cars and was buying house number seven. So the answer was a resounding no! Rang and told Mr Tromp who was in no way put out. It seemed, having spent a little more time with the minister, it turned out the cash was hotter than the inside of the hangar as he had syphoned it from public accounts and would soon be on the run. Good to know.

I told Mr Tromp to come to Zurich for a night out. Why not? He had to visit mum and son in the Netherlands so Zurich would be a good place to fly to, then either drive or take the train the rest of the way.

I know we have waxed lyrical about Zurich, but it is wonderful. Come and see me sometime, drinks on me, which at the prices here is a very generous offer. Myself and Geert had a great time and the boys were well and truly back in town. Sorry again, when it was time for us to go our separate ways. Before we did so, he'd once again brought a tonne of cash. I showed him a magic trick. There is a shop-cum-office on Bleicherweg in Zurich. Take a large amount of money inside and give it them. In return you can choose from gold bars and gold and silver coins from all countries. They never ask you any questions, they are very pleasant, and you can store your precious metals on site or if you fancy a workout, take some with you. Blondie was amazed. I told him this is legal, it is an instant cash cleaner, so begged him to stop carrying big bags of dollar bills around, please! He laughed, smiled, then proceeded to buy every precious coin in the place for his precious son. Not quite the point I was trying to make, at least he did swop some cash for bullion which he did leave in peace.

That was and is his way, so I really must get back to Sophia and Geert wants to see his son.

CHAPTER 21

Where do we go from here?

Christmas was approaching and I did not really know what to do with myself. You know me as a man who says one thing, then does another, who moans and now is about to inform you that he kind of misses the madness. I do. Anne had disappeared, not in a sinister 'we know where you live' way. She had gone up to Scotland with her friend Ruth whose father had a croft in the middle of nowhere. This is a long way of saying I could not contact her. My family were not big fans of the festive period, plus I did not fancy being cross examined about the Anne situation by my mother. We all met for a meal, exchanged some crap gifts, then went our own ways. Do not get me wrong, I welcome this attitude to 25th December. Why get stressed for a start? So, what to do? Where to go? Blondie was spending time with his family, Carmen-less.

I had money to burn and time to kill; sad to say I did not want to be all by myself. Who can I call? While we mull that over, in the interest of clarity and full transparency let's talk money.

My cut from the recent deals was quite substantial, plus I had the money from the clean deals. Forget the semantics for now anyway. If we start in Zurich, include Singapore, throw in Panama, a dash of the Cayman Isles and not forgetting France, we could say Five, Four, Three, Two, One, we may have lift-off. May also have savings in the UK plus a house in London, a house in France, Sophia, and maybe a Merc in the UK. What a...

Got a call from Gareth. Ah, that's handy. "What are you doing for Christmas and New Year?"

Great. See you in Singapore. Oh, and just to keep my promise we are going to Kula Lumpur to see in the New Year. The great thing about going to see Gareth is we go way back, so he knows where to go and what to say and not say with regards to my sadly currently separated wife.

This was supposed to be the first flight that I would have to pay for myself in a while, but with all my recent air miles the airline comped my first-class flight. What a...

A question. Do you really want to hear about me enjoying myself again? Before you answer, think back. We have been to Singapore, twice, once in depth. Also, you know me and Gareth as good friends. In the interest of full disclosure there are no women to look at this time. You know about Anne and Amanda is working on a modelling assignment in Tahiti. Maybe we should all go there! Are you that interested in KL? If you want I will stick a guide in the back. If you do want to go, just have to say the food is fab. Finally, there may be different colours and different shades and there may be a change of scene, but we know that a crisis will come so there is no real reason to wonder what will come next. So do not let your instincts betray you. Unless your memory is muddled you know we will move on to another fine mess. Heads up, Blondie and money are involved. Maybe not in the way you think, though I decided to stay in Singapore for a few weeks. Gareth had to go back to work doing that Thing he does. It is something to do with the media, IT, and involves a fair amount of travel.

He was happy enough to have me around and look after the place when he was out of town.

Please do not call me names again, but I decided to have a look round for a winter base and so spent some of the time house hunting. Quite reasonable in those days and plenty on the market, so I snapped up a place with a pool and nicely placed for all that Singapore has to offer.

Now, or was it then, I had three places to go. Nice short chapter. Will save how smug I am.

CHAPTER 22

Anything to declare, sir?

My phone was ringing; the international code on display is 0031 – the Netherlands. So you know who is calling, looks like it's time to pack and get set for another caper.

Wait a minute, I have not seen the rest of the number before. For a start it is a landline, not a mobile. Sounds like dialling code Ged. Who? He is a friend of my brothers who works for BT (other phone providers are available). His chat-up line is to ask the ladies where they are from then tell them their dialling code. Quite! Scarily, it works from time to time. Anyway, we have not digressed or procrastinated for a while. So even though inconsistency is my thing, I like to commit the same written crimes. Back to the bloody number. It may or may not be Blondie, could be one of the G-men, so I answer.

It is none of the above. For a start there is a female voice on the line. She was speaking English but was not a native speaker. The first thirty seconds or so were taken up with, "Are you Simon?"

I answered, "Yes, who are you?"

Eventfully we had a breakthrough when she told me she was a Mrs Tromp, Geert's mother.

Instead of speculating and guessing, here are the facts. Blondie, her son, was in trouble. Okay. He was in the UK. Okay. And had managed to get himself arrested and needed help. Not okay.

Guess this is the price you pay for the life you choose. I informed Gaz I was off – bit of business – packed, then hotfooted it to the airport. Holland, here we come. Managed to get a flight to Frankfurt, close enough. There was no point trying to get the finer details on the phone so it was only when Mrs T. was making me lunch the following day that the full facts emerged. Geert had manged to get himself arrested at John Lennon Liverpool Airport. It will not be a great stretch of your imagination to know why. He had a bag full of money. The only surprising thing to me was the location. Her only question was whether I could help him, as he was a good man underneath. I had no argument with that and told her so and then promised to do everything possible to get him out.

For those of you filling in the dots earlier there is some excellent news. I was on my way to Liverpool with EasyJet. Now we have had a rant about Rome, not sure the words fit but the sentiment is the same. EasyJet? More like how many ways can we make your experience and your flight difficult and uncomfortable jet. What utter bastards; from sticking my chic hand luggage in some metal frame, to complaining that the ink on my boarding piece of paper was wrong, they sucked. That was pre-flight, I had to pay for some piss-poor coffee, had my eyes assaulted by the garish interior of the plane, and was repeatedly interrupted by flight attendants trying to sell me scratch cards. You can call me what you want but please refuse to accept this low level of service and the contempt of the staff to the passengers. I do not care if it is low-cost travel, there are still basic levels of service that should be offered. Bah!

Back to Blondie who was banged up in Walton, AKA Liverpool prison. He was on remand due to the fact he had over half a million pounds on him when he arrived and Her Majesty's Custom and Excise had taken the view he may be up to no good. If only they had called his mother she would have put them right. Maybe she could represent him as well, as the court-appointed lawyer was less than useless. I had managed to get his details from the police, made an appointment and was hoping to get all the details from him. At first he did not know who Geert was. Second, he could not find the file. Eventually he managed to locate the charge sheet, which was vague to say the least. Blondie had been charged with money laundering. Oh the rich, rich irony. The police believed the money was the proceeds of crime.

The nature of the crime had yet to be established but they had narrowed it down to drug money (he is Dutch), or money with menace. Eh (protection payments because of his links to Columbia). The ever-charming Carmen would be over the moon if she knew her man was in the nick for a real crime and looked like he had grown a pair. The next item on the agenda was the defence of the client. I asked if he had seen him. No. Was there a defence plan? No. What about getting him bail? No, he is a flight risk. So there we have it, hardly Perry Mason.

First things first, I needed to get a better lawyer ASAP. Just the Yellow Pages in those days which didn't help, hence their demise. The only real criminals who may have legal counsel I knew were Dutch; one was in prison and the other three had gone to ground. That left me. The lawyers I knew were all cooperate lawyers, still better than this idiot in front of me so may as well give it a try. After a little contemplation I plumped for a guy I knew and had worked with on a share option who was from and was still based in Manchester. My theory being that all Mancunians hate Liverpudlians (Scousers). It had been quite some time since I had made a good decision; it was good to be back in the black choice wise. This was clearly my man. His name was Alastair which without me even asking, he told me meant defender of men. A good start.

After I had outlined the case, which he listened to with interest, the mere mention of Liverpool sent him into an expletive frenzy and he was practically frothing at the mouth after a very entertaining and amusing tirade. Though he specialised in corporate law, as luck would have it he had begun his career in criminal law, but had decided quite wisely there was more money and less risks drawing up contracts and smooching business types. He quickly cancelled his appointments in his diary and insisted we head over to the 'Pool to get my friend out of Walton and stick it to those lazy robbing lying Scouse bastards, could be fun!

First stop, the local magistrate to ask for bail. Her Majesty's prosecutor did not stand a chance.

He wiped the floor with him, sighting several legal precedents, establishing that Mr Tromp was an upstanding respected Dutch businessman. Still laughing, bloody brilliant. Bail was granted and we then set off for Liverpool's imposing Victorian jail. It looked scary, dirty, and dangerous from the outside so heaven knows what it is like on the inside, shudder to think.

Blondie's face was a picture when he came out of the prison. Sure he thought he was about to be deported or be fed to the British police or handed over to the Columbian authorities, which would be the scariest option as that could be a one-way ticket back to the Cali Cartel.

However, he then saw me and Alastair waiting for him in the car park and the smile just got bigger and bigger. As he was in speaking distance I got in first and said, "It is good to see you, my friend. Fancy seeing you here!" Hope the roar of laughter did not scare anybody inside the jail. It was good to see him, and considering he had been incarcerated in one of the hardest prisons in the North West of England he looked great. Immaculately dressed as always, bright eyed and bushy tailed. He hugged Alastair which came as a surprise to all concerned. Then he turned his gaze towards me. Blimey, if I had been a woman or that way inclined, it was a look of love and gratitude.

"Simon, my friend, I knew you were the right guy." BIG HUGS! As well as possibly sharing a special moment with a hug, Alastair and Geert also had something else in common. They both wanted to get out of Liverpool as fast as possible. In fact, our noble lawyer had us laughing in the car by saying the only two good things to come out of Liverpool were the M62 motorway and the East Lancashire Road. You can hear the Scouse whines from here, ay, ay, ay. Please note these are the opinions of an esteemed lawyer who, as he was born and raised in Manchester, had a black spot concerning anyone or anything that came from the Merseyside area. This is a man who thinks the Beatles are the most overrated pop group in the history of music. He thought they were four tuneless nobs who got lucky. During the journey he referred to them as the drab four. I think he may have shot John Lennon if he had got there before Mark Chapman. He then moved on to the football teams, the buildings, and the people. It was fair to say he was not a fan. He and Blondie seemed to have clicked and he told Geert to tell him all about his troubles the following day.

That night we were going to hit the north. To dubious looks from the pair of us, he said that Manchester has got everything apart from a beach. Far more accurate, as it was happening around us in a bar called Mojo, was that the city thought a table was for dancing on. When he had picked us up from the hotel at the start of our night out, he told us if he had just spent one week in Walton with the scum of the earth watching his back, he'd want to get laid. So he vowed to introduce Geert to a willing Manchester lass who would rip his balls off.

What a great guy. I had liked him instantly the first time I had met him, as after having to deal with ultra-trendy Londoners I found his attitude refreshing and his forthrightness and frankness a joy to behold. He was a straight-talking, took no prisoners (apart from Geert), in-your-face Manc.

Blondie thought he was the bees knees and was more than ready to take him up on his offer.

It looked like that offer could come to fruition at any moment as three ladies had joined our table. Kissing us all in a rather messy uncoordinated way, they then said we were all well fit and if we played our cards right we could be in for the shag of our lives. This was clearly the norm to Alastair and he ordered champagne and shouted out the top of his voice, "Oh, Manchester is wonderful." Blondie looked confused, however, after he had whispered in my ear, it seemed he was just confused about the semantics, not the situation. Though the girls could not get much work as supermodels, they were all attractive in unorthodox ways. Also though they were not exactly svelte they had curves in all the right placed and it looked like their exercise program was to have sex with men to burn off the calories from the evening's alcohol. To misquote Antony H. Wilson, "Manchester, they do things differently there."

In the interests of full disclosure, I fell off the wagon sex-wise that evening. She was one of our table trio. Her name was Lilly and she was lovely in every way. What a night, Manchester so much to answer for! The girls, actually let's call them ladies, came back to our hotel and had all hung around to join us for breakfast. While Geert and I nursed hangovers and sipped on coffee, Alastair and the ladies tucked into a full English breakfast and took it in turns to mock us, my favourite being, "Eat some breakfast, you big Dutch poof." This came from his date. Was still laughing until she asked Lilly if I was a good shag and if I had a big dick.

I was now choking on my coffee and it was Blondie's turn to laugh out loud. There is no time to go on a guilt trip over Anne as we have Geert's defence to sort out. Must get those charges dropped. The ladies said ta rah, just for the day as it was Saturday morning – we all met up that evening for more madness and much merriment. I believe Geert and Alastair swopped. Thankfully the lovely Lilly decided to give me another go as to answer her friend's question, I was a good shag, and while my penis was not the longest, it was lovely and fat (her words). Oh, how the ladies love their girth!

Have to speed along a little here with the story as the publisher is getting a bit stressed and I have missed three deadlines. Needless to say, our legal eagle put together air-tight alibies and an unbreakable defence that he called Catenaccio. The word comes from Italian and is used to describe a highly organised defence in football. How Blondie loved this, took him right back to his Watford days. Guess what? We won. All the charges were dropped and an apology was even offered and accepted. Though this was great news, during this mercifully short process by legal standards I got to spend a fair bit of time with my latest love, Lilly.

Not sure about the love bit, let's use 'like' and 'a lot'. She was good company and great fun.

Though the time was, alas, not right for either of us. On her part she loved Manchester and wanted to have fun for a few more years before settling down. On my side, please do not throw anything, but I was still in love with Anne and not over her. Plus, with Blondie as a best friend who knew what would happen next and where we would end up. Digging our way out of a bloody great big hole, no doubt. So Lilly and I parted amicably and I will always have a place in my heart for her, and still have a picture of her in my mind as she made my life so wonderful for a while.

CHAPTER 23

The bitter bank boss strikes back

After the charges were dropped we had one more memorable lads' night out in Manchester.

My two companions had long since moved on from Lilly's friends and had sampled most of what the female population of the city had to offer in our time together. Oh, how they mocked my liking of Lilly, all in good grace. By morning we had all gone our separate ways. Geert to God knows where, sure I will find out soon – that is always part of the fun. Alastair had to return to his life of cooperate drudgery, though sure he would be let out for good behaviour from time to time. It would be impossible to tie a man like him to a desk for too long as he would just dance on it. We both thanked him profusely and in turn he offered his help at the drop of a hat at any given time in the future. So once again, that left me.

I decided to do something decent for a nice change of pace and spent some quality time with my parents in the UK. Hung out with my brother and even spent some time with my sister. We love each other but find it difficult to stay in the same room together for too long. Mind you, our relationship thawed with my offer of financial assistance for an extension she was planning for her house. This time it gave me a nice glow and once more it felt good to be alive.

The bad news you can all see coming was served with dessert one evening. I was having dinner with my whole family. Usually we saved these tense affairs for unpleasant occasions like funerals and Christmas lunch. It was my idea, as feeling good to be alive, I had felt the urge to strengthen family bonds. The meal had passed relatively incident free with there being a minor scuffle at the speed at which my brother eats. He has to count his fingers after shovelling food in. My mum and I think it is funny, Dad and Sis do not. Still, no reported casualties. Over dessert, or pudding as Mrs C. number one calls it, my dad told me some bloke from the bank had called a few days ago trying to locate me. Now my father is many things and we have cleared our throats once to sing his praises, however, he has no short-term memory anymore. He forgets where he parks his car, leaves things he needs in the oddest places, and loses his house key daily. So there were no answers to who, when, and what. He just repeated that some bloke from the bank called. Even I know that can't be good news.

The following morning after speaking to some ex-colleagues, it seemed my former boss wanted to speak to me urgently about some financial mismanagement on one of my deals regarding you-know-who. Here we go again. I am not sure about you but I have just got my breath back after the latest debacle. It was not dangerous like our Columbian adventure but if you can excuse the crudeness, I was shagged out. Spending some time with my Ma and Pa had been soothing and hanging out with my unpretentious brother had been like putting the air conditioning on, on a hot day. Very refreshing! Even my sister's odd sibling resentment had been tempered by seeing her smile for the first time for what seemed like forever when the builders started work on her house thanks to her rich little brother. She also had a lovely dog called Lottie Loo who adored me. So, had spent some happy mornings in the local park near her house watching the dog chase squirrels, frolic in the fields, and in an act of brotherly love could not resist a smile when I returned her dog to her covered in mud which it proceeded to traipse though her house. Therefore, of all the worlds I was not ready to return to, my old job was top of the list.

In this situation the man to go to for some wise words was the one and only Terrence Joseph Carroll. My dad always had a fine line in advice and it was to go and see the bastard to find out what he wanted. Fair enough, my father, oh dear Father. TJC, a true gentleman in every sense of the word still missed by all who knew him. Miss you, Dad.

Trying to get into a big international bank when you no longer work there is, well, like trying to get into a large multinational financial institution. It was torture and I even threw my arms up in frustration when a security guard who had on one occasion saluted me insisted on a bag search and then the third degree on my reasons for being in the building. My parting shot was to thank him for his friendly demeanour and hope he did not go near any of our clients.

Pretty sure the big cheese had put him up to it, some may say hell hath no fury like a woman scorned. They have reckoned without the blatant bitterness of a big bad banker. The first shock (here we go again), my ex-boss had got old fast. He looked drawn, had piled the pounds on and certainly did not expect him to have grey hair. You're welcome, boss. There was no standing on ceremony and I was ushered into a conference room. Before we get into the crux of what was said, I am just trying to think what type of relationship we had before I left.

It is not exactly keeping me awake and I do not really recall it being good, as maybe he saw me as a threat. However, neither was it bad, as when my bonus was good it increased his pot. It is not that relevant so back to conference room one.

"You lying bastard, thought you were coming back? Well, you are fucked now."

Think we can assume he definitely does not like me now. In fact he informed me that I was a slippery shit and he had never liked me, and as for that stunt of walking through the office with the CEO, well, revenge was now his. He had his PC with him and, shock two, had manged to connect to the projector. His inability to master technology was legendary and the company had to pay an assistant to arrange all his PowerPoint presentations and help him with any other IT or technology issues. It was rumoured that his assistant printed off all his email messages and he read them by hand. Did wonder how many days' practicing, as he was now pacing around the room clicking and showing me various internal emails and two charts. Not sure if he knew their relevance, think BBB just wanted to milk the moment. Shock three – the objective of his presentation was that the Financial Services Authority (FSA) had recently ordered the bank to put its house in order over some rumours circulating around the financial district (The City), and shock four, they had complied. It could sometimes take years for any financial institution to do this. Their goal was to hope it went away or the people instigating the investigation died of natural causes or boredom de dum de dum. Not this time!

The FSA has a mission statement. Pah, who doesn't? Sorry, they made me put this in.

We aim to support and empower a healthy and successful financial system, where firms can thrive and consumers can place their trust in transparent and open markets.

We protect and enhance the integrity of the UK financial system. We work to ensure markets are effective, efficient and reliable.

We seek to ensure that:

Senior management are accountable for their capital markets activities, including principal and agency responsibilities.

There is a positive culture of proactively identifying and managing conflicts of interest.

There is orderly resolution and return of client assets, firms' business models, activities, controls and behaviour to maintain trust in the integrity of markets and do not create or allow market abuse, systemic risk or financial crime.

Market efficiency, cleanliness and resilience is delivered through transparency, surveillance and the supervision of infrastructures, as well as their principal users.

Firms, acting as agents on behalf of their clients, put clients' best interests at the heart of their businesses.

This was the last slide and the big bad boss's breathing was getting faster as he triumphantly informed me that my deals with those Dutch fuckers had breached one, two, and four and they would like to talk to me. The bank was giving them their full cooperation on this matter. I kept quiet but I think we all know that the fat sweaty mess in front of me was the one giving all the help the FSA needed. They wanted to see me yesterday and he was practically choking on his own self-satisfaction with his final statement of, "You'd better lawyer up."

He gave me all the contact details and as I could now see our people-friendly security guard through the glass, it was time to leave the office. Bastard never even offered me a coffee.

Hands up all those who know where this is going. Thought so. Just read chapter one if your hand was not in the air. Better give the defender of men a call.

The FSA wanted to charge me; they did not laugh when I said, "But I have not bought anything from you." To save the legal jargon it was more or less insider trading and they felt that the public should have faith in the country's financial institutions. Sure you all do. The figures they were waving around were wildly inaccurate as they were way too low. Still, might let them keep their numbers. Finally they confirm they would be approaching the CPS, the criminal prosecution service, to make formal charges. They would be asking for a custodial sentence; prison, to you and for me. Uh oh, I am in trouble. Something has come along to burst my bubble.

Not far in the dim (in the truest sense of the word), darkest past of this tome we praised Alastair's shoot-from-the-hip chat. After a cursory look through all the legal papers he did not spare me. "You're fucked." Good to know. Still admired him for this and more so when he surmised that my old boss had hung me out to dry and could have blocked the FSA questions and stopped it months ago. Still shooting, he informed me I would be eating porridge for breakfast for a while and the best he could do was cut a deal to reduce the amount I would have to stomach. So to answer a question from a long, long time ago (Chapter 1) that everyone including me has forgotten, I will get to go to prison for trying to get rich without trying. Too much, too soon, and no rules. Bugger!

Alastair got busy and told me to let my close friends and family know I would have a change of address very soon. Where to start? Anne, called, nothing, e-mail, nothing, letter, nothing; even friends and family refused to help. In a way I was pleased so just told her mother, the sainted Christine, I would be away for quite a while and to get in contact with my folks if she needed me. Which brings me to my family. Sorry Mum and Dad. Hazel cried and TJC, bless, said, "Chin up, son."

My brother and sister thought it was great, a true white-collar criminal in the family. They did this as an act of love. In the UK we do not go soft, we take the piss! So my sister's line about hoping it did not affect her extension brought the house down, though not hers. Lotty looked sad and then there was just friends to tell. Gareth laughed and said he would pop in to see me, others were shocked, and then there was only Blondie left to tell. He was deeply remorseful and offered to dial one of our emergency numbers as they would get me out of it. This showed he was a true friend because if he did dial, it would drag him back in. So I declined any form of help. His other offer of a trip of a lifetime could not be accepted as the police had my passport as part of my bail terms. Hats off to Alastair for getting bail in the first place; even the judge looked surprised when he granted it.

That left the trial, if you can call it that. Though it was in crown court there was no jury as I had pleaded guilty. Because of this there were no witnesses as the defence did not need them. The deal had been done and so all that was left was how long?

Once again, big shout out to the defender of men. The judge had more letters than Santa Claus attaining to my good character, and even more of a surprise especially to me, a list of all my charitable deeds and the good I had done in the community. He even got me a job on the off-chance the judge suspended the sentence. No chance; it was the law.

Judge Rigby seemed quite sensible and the worst thing he did on the day was to take a thirty-minute recess before passing judgment. In this time I visited the toilet three times.

All rise. "Mr Carroll you are an intelligent, hard-working man. All the letters I have read support you and praise your good character." Long pause. "However, you have broken the law and I cannot set a legal precedent by suspending any sentence given." Longer pause! "For the crime of insider trading I am sentencing you to the minimum time required by law of eight months. I do, however, recommend you serve the bulk of this sentence in an open jail. Take him down."

CHAPTER 24

At Her Majesty's Pleasure

We have not had this old chestnut for a while, so down in the holding cells waiting for the sweat box (more of this soon) you cannot help thinking, *What the hell am I doing here?*

Think we all know. First, some logistics. We were there a few pages ago. What? Okay, good point. With crime and punishment in the UK, which court you appear in and where you go if convicted are based on where the crime was committed. This was tricky in my case as there was no one place the prosecution could point to. Next, you would have where the victim came from; again, hard to put an exact location on that. Finally, which police force brought the charges. To be honest – ha, to be honest – even Alastair was confused but also delighted in the right way when it turned out I was charged by GMP. Who? Greater Manchester Police. Please, no real idea. Think it was more to do with the CPS, you remember them? The Crown Prosecution Service. No charges can be brought against anyone without their say-so, therefore my case was heard in Manchester Crown Court whose holding cells I was sitting, head in hands, suited and booted and scared. My brief had to keep it that way. Alastair gave me twenty cigs, a bag with a change of clothes, and £50 in cash. The convict kit.

Had to smile despite myself. He promised to come and see me as soon as he could, and a pat on the back. Before we get into the sweat box, an apology to my family. My mother told me she could not possibly come. My dad was a rock, also ditto our kid. My sister was the only surprise, crying like a baby. Sorry one and all, no further words as it would fail to do the situation justice.

The vans they use to transport criminals to and from court and then on to prison are quite rightly nicknamed sweat boxes. You have eight or more tiny on-board cells in the back of a fortified transit van. It is hot and you are in a box and may sweat, due to the heat or the fate that awaits. I had on an extremely expensive Savile Row bespoke suite. It had style but I'm not sure my travel companions would see it that way. Alastair told me this was a must in the court. He said, "Do not hide who you are, and by dressing well you show the court the utmost respect." I tended to agree but had asked and had been told it was not possible to change before prison.

The door to my cell opened and it was time to go. Outside the building the transport guards wanted to put handcuffs on me, which seemed a little over the top. The guy shrugged and said, Suit or no suit, you have to wear these as well." So be it. The only positive was that I was first aboard.

I sat and sweated in my little box, still unsure of

my final destination, and thought about the past. My thoughts were soon interrupted by people and noise; it seemed the van was fully booked and it was fair to say some of the passengers weren't best pleased to be on the vehicle. There was banging and screaming and two prisoners seemed to be having some sort of screaming match. Tell you, if I had a phone the big Mig or the Mob would be getting a call right about now. I just tried to tune everything out.

We got going and though you have a window of sorts, mine had been scratched with graffiti so it was difficult to get a handle on the moving landscape. In no time at all we had come to a halt. More noise and more banging, then there was even more noise as it was the destination of some of our happy travellers. Once again they were not at all happy about this. This time they may have had a point. We were in the belly of the beast, HM Prison Manchester, better known to all as Strangeways, home to some, shall we say, interesting inmates. They liked to throw the odd rooftop party, with a famous riot taking place in 1990. If folklore is to be believed it all started in the chapel, with the poor priest getting a punch on the nose for his troubles.

Three had got off so far and though I had visited the toilet several times already, would not mind another visit. Some justice, it was not Raffles, the Plaza, the Ritz, or any of the other fabulous hotels I had stayed in with my ill-gotten gains. Please don't make me get off, one more left the van so loud. Then a slam of a door, the turn of the engine, and thanks to all gods we were off again. The journey was a little longer this time and when we did finally stop I was relieved as you could be to be surrounded my far newer walls and what looked to be a fairly well equipped modern building. One of the guards who clearly saw himself as some sort of comedian said, "Welcome to HMP Forest Bank Manchester." This received a laugh from his companions and he finished with, "We will be taking you to reception to check you in one at a time." Funny, screw boy, can I borrow your phone? As I was first on it meant last off. This, like most processes to do with the running of the prison, is very slow.

After what seemed like an Ice Age it was my turn. You do go into a type of reception. It was staffed by three guards and there were two prisoners sat opposite, on my entrance. One was straight into me. "Who the fuck have you come as? Bet you're a nonce. What you fucking looking at?" Charmed.

The other inmate jumped to my defence and told him to shut it, slightly more colourfully. The prison officers then decide to intervene, saying, "Leave it Dale." First-name terms. Good service here. They then dragged off the foul-mouthed obnoxious little turd. I thanked the aforementioned Dale which seemed to surprise him, and he told me not to worry, the guy was clucking. Don't ask because I didn't.

As the prison moved so slowly I will whisk you through their entry requirements. They take your picture, take your property, give you the prison-issue clothes and cup, plate, and blanket. Then a medical. Then staggeringly, they ask you what you did and why you had been sent to them. You are then moved to a holding-cum-waiting room. Because we had been there so long a trustee prisoner brought me and Dale dinner. Thank God he laughed when asked for a wine list. More interviews; you are asked if you are suicidal, gay, or have a religious faith. Then you are taken to the induction wing. There is not much chat with the guards and due to massive overcrowding you get to spend the evening in a tiny cell with a complete stranger. My new best friend, Dale, who by the way everyone seemed to know and acknowledge, asked me to share with him. As my only choice was the angry man from reception, I chose to take up Dale on his offer. Goodnight everyone, and sleep with one eye open.

We were still banged up in the morning and as I was still alive, I asked Dale some questions. He was a professional thief and broke into upmarket properties and was working on a bit of wealth distribution. A modern-day Robin Hood, or in his own words, a Robin Bastard. Odd to say I quite liked him and at least he was honest. Yeah, yeah, semantics. I gave him a bit of my backstory, avoiding numbers and amounts. He seemed fine about this; not exactly impressed but not dismissive. He started to roll a cig and I remembered the twenty that amazingly the prison had let me keep. I dug them out of my property and this time he was impressed. He would not take them all even though they were offered. He said we can smoke some and mix some into roll-ups and trade the rest. Fine by me. He then asked if I was for real. After some clarification, 'real' being someone who does not smoke and is happy to give prison currency away gratis. Just shrugged and he smiled. His smile was not a Geert smile; for a start Blondie had teeth. Still, looked like we were cellmates. It may have been the luck of the draw but him being my pad mate was opening doors. Sadly, not the front one. Did get more toast and Dale came back with two flasks, normally only available after a month, and a TV remote.

You get the TV. Before you start your letter you do have to pay for rental. It seemed Dale was some sort of prison hard case and had a fearsome reputation if you said no to his request.

Another guy told me he would put pool balls in a sock and then try and pot them on the head of anyone who might disagree with him. Hum, the bank could use him to head up their negotiation section with the traders. Stick the fact we have a pool table in your letter too then.

Keep the pen ready. The induction wing is not too bad. It was clean, new, had worse food. Remember the roadside in Columbia? Also, most of the people on it were as scared shitless as me. The first three days was mainly going on courses of things the prison did not want you to do. Drugs, bullying, violence, stealing other convicts' stuff, and don't diss the staff and each other. It passed the time. My first disagreement was next. Thankfully I did not need Dale or his sock as it was with one of the prison officers. Some info is needed so bear with us.

Every prison in the UK has a canteen system, where you can order tobacco, sweets, drinks, toiletries, and even protein powder to help you beef up in the gym. The list gets longer and if you wait till we get to open prison, your letter will be a novel as you can order DVDs, PlayStation and radios... Great. Ha. However, the cause of row was the bloody prices. Talk about a rip-off. I thought this had been put politely and clearly; the screw mustn't have, she was so rude. For some reason I was feeling more annoyed and asked to see the governor, and asked her how people could be rehabilitated when they were being cheated by the system set up to help.

She should have worked more outside as it was like talking to a brick wall. No dice, fat cow.

Dale was now my friend for life as I asked him if he needed anything. It was nice when he said that one, I was alright and needn't get him out, and once again, was I for real? Think so. In the end he did ask me to get him some burn. Believe that is prison slang for tobacco.

It was time to move. Before we pack our bags, a tour to HMP Forest Bank Manchester. A1/A2 wings are for young offenders (YOs). It is like a zoo; people with way too much to prove down there. I think, as I cannot be bothered to check, it is 16-21, maybe 18. In prison you are not an adult until you reach 21.

B1/B2 are set aside for foreign guests. Lots of languages and the Home Office trying to kick them out. At the time, if they were from outside the EU they could be paid to leave. Don't ask.

C1/2, still laughing, are anti-drug wings and trustees. C1 is best avoided as most residents say it is where all the prison grasses are banged up.

C2, where me and Dale were off to, was the anti-drug wing. You agree to more tests and you get more perks such as gym time, out of cell time, and better job offers. More of this soon.

D1, Psychopath City. Full of real hard cases. Dale said he had been before and though he liked all the action he was trying to get some time off for good behaviour, so C2.

D2, old lags.

E1/2, induction.

F1/2, Nonce City, sex cases and paedophiles. Best not to go there.

There was also a solitary confinement if you fancied some alone time.

My new home was less salubrious than my last. Talk about false advertising. Dale insisted we clean our pad as, heaven knows what junkie scum had been it before. See? What is not to like about this guy? Then, bang up. The next day was test day and job interview day. Great. Did win some more friends as I completed four maths and five English tests so they would not be stuck on Education where the prison pay is the lowest. Then, as it is a work prison you go to HR. Pick one – Wing Cleaner, Kitchen, Workshop, Education, Packer and Admin. You then have the much sought-after orderly jobs where you get more trust, freedom, and pay. The gym is top followed by education and the library. I could not care less and told them so much, to their displeasure. There was not much they could do about it because they love to follow the rules. Therefore because of my education, work background, and my test score they gave me a job in Education helping the English teacher with the foreign nationals.

After a leisurely breakfast of toast (it is always toast, except Sunday when you get an egg as well) - what happened to porridge? - it was off to work where the commute is a riot, literally as there are running battles and chance for grudges to be settled. Your head is spinning around with all the action. The prison security is on constant manoeuvres with riot shields at the ready. They appear to love their work, smashing anyone in the vicinity. There is then a bottleneck at the entrance to the classrooms where one guy told me, "Time to get even," and smashed another prisoner's nose.

My job description was not clear. It depended on the teacher. Ken was chilled and laid back and let me wander around and help the prisoners with their letters for various appeals.

Vicky, total do-gooder, got me to help them read. Then Big John had retired, but forgot to tell the prison, so I taught and did his job. We have to go, so a description is available on request. Plus, you get a vote. A – How terrible, we must help. B – Send the bugger back!

We have to go as someone in the prison says so. It happens all the time go here; do this, such a body wants to talk. I was off to be categorised. You know I am a D, it is all at the start.

Plus, will be off to open nick in one week. The system is one transfer a week and I missed yesterday's, so six more days with the mad, mad men of the bank. At least it is Easter so I have a long weekend. Did ask about holiday pay but have yet to receive a response.

The vicar, St Steven, a true gent, had visited twice and I meant it. Even Dale said he was a good guy. He had been in the Paras and was now trying to do his bit for the lost sheep out there. Really mean it when I say he was a great man who actually did good; he was respected by everyone.

The prison had invited various dignities and charities and as Dale described, the lefty losers.

Not sure they expected to be so close to the convicts. The look on the woman's face in front of me when Dale gave her his toothless smile and said she was well fit and he would knock one out over her later. The jaws hitting the floor were far louder than any of the hymns sung.

They said one thing to us but their body language and pure discomfort was laughable. Even the Sainted Steven called them a bunch of sandal-wearing hippies who should get real. Still, it got me off the wing away from the scrounging Cat Cs. "Have you got burn, milk, a TV Guide?" and much more. There was no off switch. Even my fearsome cellmate got asked, though not for too long. I saw two of the main culprits with black eyes and spectacular bumps on their thick heads. Once again, what is not to like?

After the Easter service it was Sunday roast, sort of, then bang up. Sunday is the worst. To reduce costs and overtime the prison officers lock you up for the night as soon as they can. It is supposed to be 6pm, in reality it is 5pm. This led to a lot of soul searching in cells with some strange noises piercing the silence of the wing from time to time. Sure I heard someone being raped and this particular Sunday a scream got louder and louder, then a gurgling sound. Dale, ever the expert, informed me someone was trying to top themselves. Pause, more noise, keys, panicked shouts, silence, dead! Sorry, using the wrong tone again but what the fuck am I doing here?

He was one of my students, on the wrong wing, as he had no English and no release date.

It does not matter now, whatever the rights and wrongs he is no longer there or here!

CHAPTER 25

Holiday Camp

Before we leave the bank, forgot the great milk-nicking scandal where the thieving druggie Cat C came up with a plan to steal milk to trade. They ended up stealing from each other, and forgot where they hid it. The screws found it first. They all fell out, then grassed on each other and had a punch-up of sorts to celebrate. Madness. I was glad to be out of there. I said bye to Dale and was back in the back of the sweat box, off to HMP Kirkham category D open prison.

Dear Home Office, why is it if you trust us to wander around an open prison where you can walk out of the door, do you insist on transporting us there cooked up and handcuffed? That aside, as we swung in to Kirkham the press does have a point, as it has a feel of a holiday camp. The prisoners were walking around free, enjoying the late April sunshine, and there was a relaxed air to the place. This time they let us all out at the same time and I could smell fresh air for the first time in two or so weeks; it was not quite San Diego but you could smell a scent of sea air and fresh cut grass.

No need to bring back our favourite question; this place may be bearable, it was. The guards at reception and the stores were polite and efficient and the billet cleaner even paused his computer game to give me some toilet paper and show me round my room and give me the lay of the land.

My room was the last on the left, so my new home was Billet D room 10. Nice enough. Mike, as that was his name, then gave me the run-down on my neighbours and himself. He was ex-army (quite a few inside) and had got involved in selling off army surplus. We had a guy who imported tobacco but forgot to pay tax and got nicked at Dover with 100,000 without any paperwork. Another guy forged cash, a benefit fraudster. A few drunk drivers and a bank robber who had ticked all the boxes and managed to become Cat D. All in all, a good bunch. No begging – we shared, no grassing, and self-policing.

When they came in from work all introduced themselves and it seemed I was going to fit right in. Like most prisons the next day was induction day; less stress and my new job was a gym orderly. How this happened, no one knew. I didn't want it, I didn't ask for it, but the Senior Officer (SO) decided I would be perfect, so much so one of his team came to get his marker in first before the library or education could get me. This was all very nice except this was one of the most sought-after jobs available. You could train when you wanted, could wander around the prison, got your meals earlier and could do all manner of courses that did help. For example, the guys in there learned first aid, got an FA coaching badge, physio, and some became gym trainers on release. True rehabilitation. The downside was the local community could use all the facilities and in the afternoon local stroke victims would come for courses and the prisoners had to hold their hand. I enjoyed this but I was alone.

Forgot the downside. Curtis Warren wanted my job. He was/is quite a famous Liverpool gangster, importer and exporter of drugs, bloody huge, and had a bit of a temper. 'What the hell was he doing here?' is our new question. Mick pointed him out to me and even came over to do the introductions. Mick was clearly in awe and I think even asked to feel his bicep – yuk. Finally we got down to business. Thank the god of Kirkham, he was more than fine and wished me luck and said he had heard of me, which was a huge surprise. Still, all was well. However, it meant Mick was now asking me all manner of questions and he was not alone, with the whole billet joining in before lunch. Shrugged it all off and claimed a case of mistaken identity. The regime at Kirkham was (get that pen out again) great. A good breakfast thanks to Pops. He was my neighbour who just happened to work in the kitchen and gave me extra portions and brought back fruit and other goodies. In turn I ordered him burn and paid for his newspaper at the weekend. Quid pro quo as they say. Well, I would.

After breakfast it was off to work. No traffic, overcrowding, just a leisurely walk to the huge gym. After setting up for the day you could sleep if you wanted or find something to do. No pressure. The people I worked with were funny and once you got to know them the officers were a hoot. There is a lot at the back so here is the SP. There was Mr Warring, the senior officer; he like to be called SO. Eddie, another orderly, explained he was an ex-para, hard as nails but straight and fair. He was, and would talk to you as a colleague and all the staff and cons respected him. Then his number two, Mr P. (Proctor); he claimed to hate everyone and everything, and was rude to all the prisoners. Deep down he had a dark sense of humour and the lads loved him. I gave him pension advice and sorted out the SO's finances.

Two more. Fez, a gym junkie who would challenge all comers and win. He beat me at badminton in his wellington boots. Finally, PJ (Peter Jones), an easy-going officer who coached the football team, no away games.

All the officers loved their jobs. No hassle, good salary with pension guarantees. Plus all the on-the-job training meant they all had outside interests and had other income. Easy hours and so the job was great. You received a special badge and could go anywhere in the prison.

Eddie and I marked out the football field and running tracks in the early May sun and the lads played tennis or squash. You could train when you wanted and you got your meals first. All the juiced-up prisoners used to offer you all manner of things to reserve weights and the rest of the prison revered you.

Final workout for your pen. There were two snooker tables, twelve pool tables, badminton and squash courts. There was a sauna and a satellite TV room for the football. My personal favourite was the crown green bowling green in the centre of the prison and finally the lake-cum-pond where you could fish. So it did amaze me that some prisoners would moan and some idiots managed to get shipped out to real stir. Why? GOK only knows. This was normally for drugs or phones though.

Pat, a lovely if somewhat trusting guy in for drug running, sounded cool. Nah, he was used. He loved the wildlife and he fed the ducks and had named them. He could be considered a simple soul but he brought peace and harmony to all around him. Sadly some nasty skanky C who had somehow been put on the freedom bus to HMP Kirkham thought it would impress people to feed the ducks burgers. He'd been mocking Pat but got the shock of his life when he beat the living crap out of him and chucked him in the pond. Sadly this meant the genial gent was asked to leave. The skank begged to go as there was a huge price on his horrible zit face.

Everyone else who got in bother was, of course, innocent, so one of my side lines was writing letters of appeal and letters to the governor to ask him not to send them back to bang up.

After a few early successes, my inbox was overflowing. Our billet was a happy place so I always shared my gifts. Curtis would always say hello and Eddie told me I was the real deal. So Dale asked if I was for real, and Eddie thinks I am the real deal. Strange. The shrug usually did the trick, keep the mystery. This was not fool proof and the bank robber pushed me on my crimes one day and gave a little away.

It turned out he just wanted some investment advice; he gave me some expensive sportswear as payment and unfortunately it raised my profile a little more than I had anticipated, but I managed to convince most that I was pure white collar. Hope you have sent your letter because what follows does not belong in it, as I was proud of some of the things inside. I ran a 10km for charity in a very good time, helped Davis, a civilian, with his recovery from a stroke, helped other prisoners with their education and always shared my wealth. My health was good, I was the fittest I'd been for years, and had caught up on my reading.

Finally, you do need to know that the level of intellect and quality of debate and conversation was amazing. Go on, you ask. Were you happy? Oh yes. Guess who has written and asked me for a visiting order (VO) No need, is there? Blondie will be with us very soon. All of my family had visited and so I was happy when my Dad told me I had not been bad, just made a mistake. He was convinced of this due to the surroundings. "This is a bloody holiday camp, son."

My brother loved it and wanted a who's who guide to the criminals. Other friends came and even Gareth flew in, great gesture but the combination of his flash car and flash clothes and demeanour did not help me stay under the radar.

Of course Alastair came and he drummed up a few new clients, think he was bored of business law. That left only one man.

CHAPTER 26

We've got to get you out of this place

I was just thinking to myself about why when Geert is around trouble is not far behind. You may rightly wonder why I was always pleased to see him. I feel we have done this before but do have to repeat how much fun he is to be around. Also, things are never dull and you are never sure who or what is around the corner. There is some danger but it adds to the flavour.

He is very generous and has style, and the sun always seems to be out when he was around.

Visits are much easier than in normal prisons and take place Saturday and Sunday, though legal and social worker visits can come in the week. The Sunday Blondie breezed in the room was full and until his entrance everyone else was deeply involved in their own conversations. He shook hands with the officers on duty, gave the lady in the café a twenty pound tip and then shook hands with Curtis who was the star-struck one for a change. Oh no, he knew him, there will be questions. No time as the smile is blinding me. "Hello, my friend." You cannot help but smile back. We exchanged pleasantries but I had to know how he knew Curtis. He told me he knew his boss and had had been introduced to Mr Warren a few times. Believe a rebuttal may be required. First, hard to believe that Curtis had a boss. Second, who was he and how did Blondie know him? Here we go. "Well, you know that £500k? It was his change from a deal with Miguel and I was just tidying up."

What?

"Carmen asked as a favour for Miguel!"

At this point while shaking my head he told me there is an irony of sorts and we had a great few weeks thanks to his money transfer, and don't forget lovely Lilly. Bloody hell, he had done it again. I laughed so loud a prison officer asked if I was okay. He smiled again and we had a nice trip down Memory Lane. We sure had lived. He then asked about the conditions and was puzzled about the lack of ladies. I did mention the latest prison gossip that a female officer had just been fired. Her crime was going into selected inmates' rooms and spreading the love. Unfortunately she had started to shag the same guy. While this may be more monogamous, it meant it was easier to get caught. I am not sure what her or the inmate's crime was but she was fired, and rather unfairly in my opinion, her conquest was shipped out to a harsher regime. Speaking of harsh, in my opinion the biggest crime was how ugly she was and how desperate the prisoner must have been.

Now Geert was laughing. We chatted more and I'm sure you are wondering why our dodgy

Dutchman has come to visit. We know he is a good guy deep down, we know he is a good friend, but, and make that big, what does he want? Well, here goes.

You are allowed up to two hours and after about ninety of those the enigmatic Erasmus told me he needed to talk to me. Believe it or not, this does make sense. All prison visiting rooms in the UK are bugged so you do have to be careful. He asked if that would be possible. Again, not a daft question. If you make it to open prison, after a short time period you are entitled to home or town visits. Home was out of the question as mine was too far and would not be allowed anyway. I did not want to put my parents through any more so told him to contact Alastair and get him to request a town visit with the choice of Preston or Blackpool.

Geert had heard of Blackpool so we agreed to meet in Preston; it could be next Saturday or two weeks at the most. We spent the last twenty minutes or so generally having a great time.

Without wishing to sound weird, I was sad when our time was up. One, it was fun, and two, all the bloody questions that other inmates now had. Curtis was the first and wanted to know way too much. Of course quite a few people saw me with him and they continued. Even the gym staff were curious. Not sure why, as what I told everyone was the truth, my part was just to move money around. Yeah, but whose money? Always said I never really knew. Not sure many bought that but at least I wanted for nothing the following week. Cons were falling over themselves to give me stuff.

Alastair waved his wand and I had a town visit

with Geert booked for the following Saturday. I have just remembered that I have broken one law. I flew straight to Liverpool to help Geert. Still, only EasyJet, let's go to Preston.

Alastair picked me up and in the car asked what I was up to. Think he believed me when I told him nothing. Think my shrug helped as it was almost epileptic. His only condition was that he didn't care what I did in the future, but please be in the car park at 4pm so he could take me back, and far more importantly he did not have to take my place. Blondie was there to meet us and gave Alastair his word that we would both be back at this point at 4pm. It was 10am so the First question was, what the hell we were going to do in Preston all day? Turns out, nothing. Geert had taken a liking to Manchester so the first thing we did was go to his car and set off. I told him to drive slowly as we may overtake my lawyer and the shock could cause some sort of collision. Once ensconced in an upmarket café in the centre of the city Blondie doled out his woes. He had fucked up, Todd style. My eyes started to roll, but I did ask how.

He had moved most of Miguel's and some of the Americans' cash into Spain. "Why?"

Apparently the Spanish are easy to bribe, speak the same language as our Columbian chums, and most importantly they did not ask questions. So one might ask, what was the problem?

Well the cash-loving Dutchman had changed all the dosh into the soon to be discontinued Spanish Pesetas. My eyes were now closed. During the last three months he had kept his head down, trying to be a good father, staying away from Carmen and living a quiet if good life. Of course this could not last so here we are again ready to run into the unknown. The problem was, run and unknown meant more to me. Kirkham was a holiday camp plus I did not have that long left – five months or so. My family had forgiven me and I hoped to come out a better person.

Blondie cut in and had already read my mind, and said he wished he could wait till my release but he needed me now. Head back now and I let out a groan. "My friend, there is too much cash and not enough time." At what point does a man say enough is enough? I was close and told my friend so. He sympathised and he told me in my position he would have walked away before now. He did have one last card to play and to his credit was reluctant to do so. When I say card, that should be corrected to cards. The Jack of Boredom, the Queen of Excitement, the King of Friends and the Ace of Adventure. Damn! Looks like I am all in for another bumpy ride. Writing, or typing if we are being closer to our friend's semantics, hard to believe, I know. However, remember Mrs Sumner's advice? Write what you know! So here we stand. The only thing you now need to know is how to escape from an open prison. Well, you cannot jump over the wall as there isn't one.

You can just walk out of the front door, though they may ask why. We had both ruled out Not coming back from the town visit as the defender of men would be in need of himself. So what to do? Blondie had a plan, doesn't he always? He had noticed the lack of security on his last visit and that no one had checked IDs or who was who when you come in and out.

Remember, this is a true story and has not just been done in open nick. Find two people who need extra cash, send them a VO – one swops places with you, and you walk out with the other. At worst they get three months in prison themselves if a man. If of the female persuasion they claim a crime of passion and get a slap on the wrists. Please do not rush to Google, Perverting the Cause of Justice and quibble. I speak from experience, Can we order one man and a lady, please? Make the woman Maria or Carmen Lopez. Alas, no, though I did get our order by the following week's visiting time – very efficient.

A very attractive blonde lady who on arriving engaged me in a bout of tonsil tennis, and good old Geert had found someone, while not exactly a stunt double could fool my family on a dark night. Good work, Dutchman. As simple as that, I now have 'escape from prison' on my CV. Did not mention the 'open' bit as it's not that impressive and is more like a walk in the park or a walk into the car park in this case. There to meet me was Geert and his grin, so two Blondies and me. Get the motor running, head out to the highway, looking for adventure, in whatever comes our way.

Like two of nature's children we were born, born to be wild. May just pop to the toilet at the service station first, what with all the excitement and all.

Before we head off into the sun there is a bit of tidying up to do. Hard as it may be to believe, I would miss my job and some of the people. You cannot exactly say goodbye in these situations, so farewell to SO Warring, Fez, PJ, and Proctor or Mr P to his friends – one by my count. Good luck to Eddie; you are welcome to all my stuff, even ordered some burn and paid for your newspapers for the last six months of your sentence. Bye to Billet D, a good bunch. Even if we all chose the wrong route deep down you are all alright. Good luck especially to Pops. Hope you stay with the treatment, Davies. Think you are close to a breakthrough.

Finally, an apology to Alastair; hope there are no comebacks or repetitions, know you will see the funny side. What more apologies? Mum, Dad, Andrew, Nicola, and Lottie, do not expect you to understand, I don't. Call it friendship, loyalty, or blind stupidity, I still love you. Do hope to make amends one day. Anyone else? No. Good, because now we are off to sunny Spain. Y Viva España.

CHAPTER 27

Don Simon arrives at last!

The blonde who had kindly stuck her tongue down my throat was called Anika, a delight. We had the pleasure of her company till Scotland, then like most good things she was gone.

Wait a minute, wait a minute. Scotland? Aren't we off to Spain?

Please remember your rules.

We said, "See you,' to Jimmy, then, "What about you?"

To Northern Ireland then to Dublin. Party!

We were due to fly from that fair city but a paranoid Geert seemed to think there were some familiar faces at the airport. So we drove south and faced a very long boat journey. Cork to Roscoff. Fortunately we both had our sea legs on. At last we had made in to France and the future. So uncertain, and who knows about the end. Downhill all the way to Spain from here.

It was a great drive though. We have done the west coast of the USA, Italy, and now we have the west coast of France before us. Places of interest should you ever find your way out here are as follows.

Quimper, magical at dusk. Carnac for the stones, smaller but far more random than Stonehenge. The Oxford Bar in the Vendee, full of nubile young travel reps. Bordeaux, of course, and Blondie and I had a bash at surfing in Biarritz. He of course had the balance of a ninja, while I had all the poise of an elephant on roller skates. A bad analogy but I hope you get my drift. Then back to life. Back to reality. Miguel had called the devil woman who had spoken in tongues to Geert. The gist of which – was the cash okay?

Some Russian had sent Blondie an e-mail. Was the cash okay? A former Nigerian minister Currently in exile awaiting extradition. Was the cash alright? We are artists so just trying to paint the picture. The cash was alright and okay, however, it had six months to change its image. Blondie wasn't worried. Why? He had me. Great. The G-men were on the way, that is great, and we had been here before.

Some minor problems. Me, for one. The FSA had blacklisted me so it would be difficult if not impossible to trade. The G-men were officially retired and knew no one in Spain. Geert had Carmen hovering like a vulture from afar. Last but not least, all of the people listed above were not known for their patience and tolerance of mistakes.

Our base was Barcelona, one of the homes to the great deeds of Mr Cruyff. We will need some magic, that is for sure. Blondie's brilliant plan was for us to go undercover so to speak. Or in his words, hide in plain sight. Vinny – hey, Vinny's back – said, "What? Find fucking jobs." It seemed so. Blend in, fade away and then ch-ch-ch-changes of cash was what we were looking for.

Hoping to be different men, Jan got a job at the port, HB the airport, and Vinny somehow got a job for the local tourist board. They were the manual labour, nothing fancy or clever. Their job was to exchange as much cash without drawing attention to them or us. This was going to take a while. However, all had the ability to find ways to do this plus try to find others who may help. That left me and Mr Tromp. His bright idea was to find work in the best hotel in town in order to meet the movers and shakers in the city.

That left yours truly. My job was to find a job that would leave my time to tap up old contacts, Jean Pierre being one, contact our French company in Reims, and pop in and out of town. That meant a job with easy hours and lots, and lots of holidays. Saw an ad on the window of a nondescript building. 'Teach English to children, teenagers and some adults.'

No qualifications or experience required but needed urgently. Sounds fine to me. Fifteen hours a week, plenty of time to blend in and try and change the cash. Now we all have work and the huge pile of shit, or Pesetas if you prefer, is slowly changing to the Euro. Sorry to complain but it was not looking good. There was bloody tonnes of cash and hard as it is to believe, all of us were truly sick of the sight of all that money. Call it justice, if you will.

My job, if you can call it that, started on the

Monday. The previous incumbent had had a break down and fled. Not surprised, my first class was a bunch of hyperactive five-year-olds. Little bastards. Next, eleven to thirteen, pre-pubescent and confused, and finally the disaffected fifteen-year-olds way too cool for school. The three-hour day felt like thirty. Blondie's job sucked; there was just no respect these days. The G-men were grim and that cash pile was still ever present.

My job was the worst by far. Horrible buggers. I hated them, but like cats they knew and for some perverse reason they loved me. Who knows the mind of a child? I was rude, made them work, made fun of the troubled teens and became a drill sergeant – pesky kids.

Vinny and Jan had visions of shadowy figures tailing them, Bosch was going mad, and the Smile was straightening by the day. Another day surrendered to self-preservation. The kids calling loud from above. Blondie was stuck with others who care for themselves, Vinny was in fear of every day and every evening, HB was being called from above, and Jans was finding changing cash was a painstaking devotion to the money he loved. Guess we had done this for a reason, maybe a blindness that had touched us like a perfection, but was now hurting like everything else. That day the kids found out my name was Simon. A popular juice and wine in these parts is named Don Simon. Kids. Ha. My name is now Don Simon!

An extremely unsatisfying ending in so many ways. So let me leave you with the words of another. Slightly paraphrased and like everything else, stolen or lost.

Family, I tried. Please believe me, I'm doing the best that I can. I'm ashamed of the things I've been put through, I'm ashamed of the person I am. But if you could just see the beauty, these things I could never describe. These pleasures a wayward distraction. That is my one lucky prize!

That is the end for now. This is the price you pay for the life you choose! Isolation.